THE SILVER MASK

Also by

HOLLY BLACK *and*
CASSANDRA CLARE

THE IRON TRIAL

THE COPPER GAUNTLET

THE BRONZE KEY

MAGISTERIUM

BOOK FOUR

THE SILVER MASK

HOLLY BLACK *and* CASSANDRA CLARE

WITH ILLUSTRATIONS BY
SCOTT FISCHER

SCHOLASTIC PRESS / NEW YORK

Library of Congress Cataloging-in-Publication Data available

ISBN 978-0-545-52236-6

10 9 8 7 6 5 4 3 2 1   17 18 19 20 21

Printed in the U.S.A.   23
First edition, October 2017

Book design by Christopher Stengel

FOR ELIAS DELOS CHURCHILL,
WHO MAY BE THE EVIL TWIN

↑ ≈ △ ○ @

CHAPTER ONE

PRISON WAS NOT like Call expected it to be.

He had grown up with the crime shows on television, so he thought he was supposed to have a gruff roommate to show him the ropes and how to get really buff from lifting weights. He was supposed to hate the food and not start anything with anybody, for fear of getting shanked with a cleverly sculpted toothbrush knife.

It turned out that the only thing being in magical prison had in common with television prison was that the main character was totally framed for a crime he hadn't committed.

In the mornings, he was awoken when lights all over the Panopticon went from dim to blindingly bright. Blinking and yawning, he watched the other prisoners (there seemed to be around fifty) as they were let out of their cells. They shuffled off, probably to breakfast, but Call's tray was delivered right to his door by two guards, one of whom scowled. The other looked intimidated.

Call, who had grown bored over the last six months, made a face just to see the freaked-out guard get more freaked-out.

None of them saw him as a fifteen-year-old, as a kid. They all thought of him as the Enemy of Death.

In all the time he'd been here, not a single person had come to visit him. Not his father. Not his friends. Call tried to tell himself that they weren't allowed, but that wasn't comforting either; they were probably in a lot of trouble. They probably wished they'd never even heard of Callum Hunt.

He finished eating some of the slop on the tray and then brushed his teeth to get the taste out of his mouth. The guards returned — it was time for interrogation.

Every day, he was taken to a windowless, white-walled room where three Assembly members grilled him about his life. It was the only interruption in the monotony of his day.

What was your first memory?

When did you realize you were evil?

I know you say that you can't remember anything about being Constantine Madden, but what if you try harder?

How many times did you meet Master Joseph? What did he say to you? Where is his stronghold? What are his plans?

Whatever his answer, they would go over the minutia until Call himself got confused. They accused him of lying a lot.

Sometimes when he got tired and bored, he was tempted to lie because what they wanted to hear was so obvious and it seemed like it might be easier to tell them. But he didn't lie, because his Evil Overlord list was back in effect and he was assigning himself points for anything he did that seemed Evil Overlord–ish. Lying definitely counted.

It was easy to rack up Evil Overlord Points in prison.

His interrogators talked a lot about the devastating charm of the Enemy of Death and how Call shouldn't be allowed to talk to any of the other prisoners, for fear of seducing them over to his evil schemes.

Call might have found this flattering if it wasn't so clear that they thought he was deliberately hiding this aspect of his character from them. If Constantine Madden had possessed devastating charisma, they felt Call was showing the exact opposite. They didn't look forward to seeing him — and he didn't look forward to seeing them, either.

That day, though, Call was in for a surprise. When he walked in to be interrogated, it wasn't his usual interrogators sitting there. Instead, on the other side of the white desk, he found his former teacher, Master Rufus, dressed in black, his bald brown head shining under the too-bright lights.

Call hadn't seen anyone he knew in so long. He had an urge to leap across the table and hug Master Rufus, despite the fact that Master Rufus was glowering at him and wasn't a huge hugger in general.

Call sat down in the chair opposite his teacher. He couldn't even wave or offer to shake Master Rufus's hand, since his wrists were bound in front of him with a glowing chain of incredibly hard metal.

He cleared his throat. "How's Tamara?" he said. "Is she all right?"

Master Rufus looked at him for a long time. "I'm not sure I should tell you," he said finally. "I am not sure who you are, Call."

Call's chest hurt. "Tamara's my best friend. I want to know how she is. And Havoc. Even Jasper."

It felt strange not to mention Aaron, too. Despite knowing Aaron was dead, despite going over the circumstances of his death again and again — Call still missed him in a way that made him much more present than he was absent.

Master Rufus steepled his fingers under his chin. "I want to believe you," he said. "But you've lied to me for a long time."

"I didn't have a choice!" Call protested.

"You did. You could have told me at any time that Constantine Madden lived inside you. How long did you know? Did you trick me into choosing you as an apprentice?"

"At the Iron Trial?" Call couldn't believe it. "I didn't know anything back then! I tried to fail — I didn't even *want* to go to the Magisterium."

Master Rufus still looked skeptical. "It was the fact you tried to fail that caught my eye. Constantine would have known that. He would have known how to manipulate me."

"I'm not him," said Call. "I might have his soul, but I'm not him."

"Let us hope not, for your sake," said Rufus.

Call felt bone-tired all of a sudden. "Why did you come?" he asked his teacher. "Because you hate me?"

This seemed to take Master Rufus aback for a moment. "I don't hate you," he said with more sadness than anger. "I came to like Callum Hunt — very much. But, once, I liked Constantine Madden . . . and he nearly destroyed us all. Perhaps that's why I came: to see if I can trust myself as a judge of character . . . or if I've made the same mistake twice."

He looked as tired as Call felt.

"They're done interrogating you," Rufus continued. "Now they have to decide what to do with you. I intended to speak at the hearing, to say what you just said — that you may have Constantine's soul, but you are not Constantine. Still, I had to see it myself to believe it."

"And?"

"He was much more charming than you."

"So everyone says," muttered Call.

Master Rufus hesitated. "Do you want to get out of prison?" he asked.

It was the first time anyone had asked Call that.

"I don't know," he said after some thought. "I — I let Aaron get killed. Maybe I deserve to be here. Maybe I should stay."

After this admission, there was a long, long silence. Master Rufus rose to his feet. "Constantine loved his brother," he said.

"But he would never have said he deserved to be punished for his brother's death. It was always someone else's fault."

Call didn't say anything.

"Secrets hurt the keeper more than you think. I always knew you had secrets, Callum, and I'd hoped you'd reveal them to me. If you had, maybe things would have gone differently."

Call closed his eyes, afraid that Master Rufus was right. He'd kept his secrets and then he'd made Tamara and Aaron and Jasper keep them, too. If only he'd gone to Master Rufus. If only he'd gone to someone, maybe things would be different.

"I know you still have secrets," Master Rufus went on, surprising Call into looking up.

"So you think I'm lying, too?" Call demanded.

"No," Master Rufus said. "But this may be your last chance to unburden yourself. And it may be my last chance to be able to help you."

Call thought of Anastasia Tarquin and how she'd revealed herself as Constantine's mother. At the time, he hadn't known what to think. He was reeling from Aaron's death, reeling from feeling like everyone he'd believed in had betrayed him.

But what good was telling Master Rufus that? It wouldn't help Call. It would only hurt someone else, someone who'd put her trust in him.

"I want to tell you a story," Master Rufus said. "There was a mage, once, a man who very much liked teaching and sharing his love of magic. He believed in his students and he believed in himself. When a great tragedy shook that belief, he realized he was lonely — that he had dedicated all his life to the Magisterium and that it was otherwise empty."

Call blinked. He felt pretty sure this story was about Master Rufus himself, and he had to admit he'd never thought of Rufus as having a life outside the Magisterium. He'd never thought about Rufus having friends or a family or anyone to visit on holidays or make tornado phone calls to.

"You can just say this story is about you," Call told his teacher. "It'll still have emotional resonance."

Master Rufus glared at him. "Fine," he said. "It was after the Third Mage War that I faced the loneliness of the life I had chosen. And as fate would have it, I fell in love soon after — in a library, researching ancient documents." He smiled a little. "But he wasn't a mage. He knew nothing of the secret world of magic. And I couldn't tell him. It would have broken all the rules if I'd told him how our world worked, and he would have thought I was insane. So I told him that I worked abroad and came home for holidays. We spoke often, but essentially, I was lying to him. I didn't want to be, but I was."

"Isn't that a story about how it's better to keep secrets?" Call asked.

Master Rufus's eyebrows made another of their unlikely moves, lowering in a truly impressive glower. "It's a story meant to show you that I understand about keeping secrets. I understand how they protect people and how they can hurt the person keeping them. Call, if there's anything to tell, tell me, and I will do whatever I can to make sure it helps you."

"I don't have any secrets," Call said. "Not anymore."

Master Rufus nodded, then sighed.

"Tamara is fine," he told Call. "Lessons without you and Aaron are lonely, but she is coping. Havoc misses you, of course. As for Jasper, I could not guess. He has done some strange things with his hair lately, but that might have nothing to do with you."

"Okay," Call said, a little dazed. "Thanks."

"As for Aaron," said Master Rufus, "he was buried with all the splendor accorded a Makar. His funeral was attended by the entire Assembly and all of the Magisterium."

Call nodded and looked at the floor. *Aaron's funeral.* Hearing Master Rufus say those words — hearing the pain in his voice — made it feel more than real to Call. This would always be the central fact of his life: If it hadn't been for him, his best friend would still be alive.

Master Rufus headed for the door to let himself out, but he paused on the way, just a second, and rested his hand on Call's head. It made Call's throat tighten up in a way that surprised him.

When Call was escorted back to his cell, he had the next surprise of the day. His father, Alastair, was standing outside, waiting for him.

Alastair gave a little wave, and Call wiggled his cuffed

hands. He had to blink a lot or the devastatingly villainous charms of the Enemy of Death were going to dissolve into tears.

Call's guards brought him into his cell and uncuffed him. They were older mages, dressed in the dark brown uniform of the Panopticon. After undoing his hands, they fastened a metal cuff around his leg, one that connected to a hook in the wall. The chain was long enough to allow Call to wander around the cell, but not long enough for him to reach the bars or the door.

The guards left the cell, locked it, and retreated into the shadows. Call knew they were there, though. That was the point of the Panopticon: Someone was always watching you.

"You're all right?" said Alastair roughly, as soon as the guards were gone. "They haven't hurt you?"

He looked as if he wanted to grab Call up and run his hands over him for injuries, the way he used to when Call fell off a swing set or knocked into a tree on his skateboard.

Call shook his head. "They haven't tried to hurt me physically at all," he said.

Alastair nodded. His eyes looked pinched and tired behind his glasses. "I would have come sooner," he said, settling himself on the uncomfortable-looking metal chair the guards had placed on the other side of the bars, "but they weren't allowing you visitors."

The wash of relief Call felt was incredible. Somehow he had managed to convince himself that his father was happy they'd locked him up. Or maybe not *happy* — but better off without him.

He was so glad that wasn't true.

"I tried everything," Alastair told his son.

Call didn't know how to respond. There was no way for him to say how sorry he was. He also didn't understand why all of a sudden he was allowed to have visitors . . . unless he'd outlived his usefulness to the Assembly.

Maybe these were the last visits he'd ever have.

"I saw Master Rufus today," he told his dad. "He said they were done interrogating me. Does that mean they're going to kill me?"

Alastair looked shocked. "Call, they can't do that. You haven't done anything wrong."

"They think I murdered Aaron!" Call said. "I'm in prison! Obviously, they think I did something wrong."

And I did *do something wrong*, he added in his head. Even if Alex Strike had been the one to actually kill Aaron, keeping Call's secret was the reason he was dead.

Alastair shook his head, dismissing Call's words. "They are afraid — afraid of Constantine, afraid of you — so they're looking for an excuse to keep you here. They don't really believe you were responsible for Aaron's death." Alastair sighed. "And if that doesn't comfort you, think of this — since they don't understand how Constantine transferred his soul to you, I am sure they don't want to risk you transferring your soul to someone else."

Call's dad hated the mage world and wasn't much of an optimist to begin with, but in this case, Alastair's grimness made Call feel better. He definitely had a point. It had never even occurred to Call that he could transfer his soul to someone else, or that the mages might be worried about it.

"So they're going to keep me here, locked up," Call said. "And then they're going to throw away the key and forget me."

Alastair was silent for a long moment after that, which was a lot less reassuring.

"When did you know?" Call blurted out, afraid the silence might drag on longer.

"Know what?" Alastair asked.

"That I wasn't your real son."

Alastair frowned. "You *are* my son, Callum."

"You know what I mean," Call said with a sigh . . . although he couldn't deny that it made him feel better that Alastair had corrected him. "When did you realize I had his soul?"

"Early," Alastair said, surprising Call a little. "I guessed. I knew what Constantine had been studying. It seemed possible he had succeeded in shifting his soul into your body."

Callum remembered the damning message his mother had left for Alastair, the one that Master Joseph, the Enemy of Death's instructor and most devoted minion, had shown him, but that his father had left out of his story:

KILL THE CHILD.

It still chilled him to think of his mother writing that with her dying strength, of his father reading those words with a squalling baby — Call — in his arms.

Alastair could have just walked out of the cave if he guessed what it meant. The cold would have done the rest.

"Why did you do it? Why did you save me?" Callum demanded now. He hadn't meant his words to sound so angry, but they did. He *felt* angry, even though he knew the alternative was his own death.

"You're my son," Alastair said again, helplessly. "Whatever else you are, you are always and also my child. Souls are malleable, Call. They're not set in stone. I thought if I raised you correctly . . . if I gave you the right guidance . . . if I loved you enough, you would be all right."

"Look how that turned out," Call said.

Before his dad could answer, a guard reappeared in front of the cell to announce that visiting time was over.

Alastair stood up and then, in a low voice, spoke again. "I don't know if I did any of the right things, Call. But for what it's worth, I think you turned out fine."

With that, he walked away, escorted by another guard.

↑ ≈ △ ○ @

Call slept better that night than he had since his first night in the Panopticon. The bed was narrow and the mattress flat, and it was cold in the cell. At night, when he closed his eyes, he always had the same dream: the bolt of magic hitting Aaron.

Aaron's body sailing through the air before it hit the ground. Tamara crouched over Aaron, sobbing. And a voice saying, *It's your fault; it's your fault.*

That night, though, he didn't dream, and when he woke up, there was a guard outside his cell, holding his tray of breakfast. "You've got another visitor," the guard said, looking at Call sideways. He was pretty sure all the guards were still waiting for him to slay them with that charisma.

Call sat up. "Who is it?"

The guard shrugged. "Some student from your school."

Call's heart began to pound. It was Tamara. It had to be Tamara. Who else would visit him?

He barely noticed the guard sliding the breakfast tray through the narrow opening at the bottom of the door. He was too busy sitting up straight and running his fingers through his tangled hair, trying to calm it and figure out what to say to Tamara when she came in.

Hey, how are you doing, sorry I let our best friend get killed. . . .

The door opened and his visitor came through, walking between two guards. It was a Magisterium student — that was true.

But it wasn't Tamara.

"Jasper?" Call said in disbelief.

"I know." Jasper held up his hands as if to ward off gratitude. "Obviously you're overwhelmed by my kindness in coming here."

"Uh," Call said. Master Rufus had been right about

Jasper — his hair looked like he hadn't brushed it in years. It was sticking out all over. Call marveled at it. Had Jasper really worked to get it looking like that? On purpose? "I assume you came to tell me how much everyone at school hates me."

"They don't think of you all that much," Jasper said, obviously lying. "You just didn't make that big of an impression. Mostly, everyone's sad about Aaron. They thought of you as his sidekick, you know? Blending into the background."

They think of you as his murderer. That's what Jasper meant, even if he didn't say it.

After that, Call couldn't bring himself to ask about Tamara. "Did you get in a lot of trouble?" he asked instead. "I mean, because of me."

Jasper rubbed his hands against his designer jeans. "Mostly they wanted to know if you put spells on us to keep us in your dark thrall. I said you weren't a good enough mage to do anything like that."

"Thanks, Jasper," said Call, not sure if he meant it or not.

"So what's it like in the ole Panopticon?" Jasper asked, looking around. "It's very, uh, sterile-looking in here. Have you met any real criminals? Did you get a tattoo?"

"Seriously?" Call said. "You came to ask me if I got a tattoo?"

"No," said Jasper, abandoning all pretenses. "I actually came because — well — Celia broke up with me."

"What?" Call was incredulous. "I can't believe it."

"I know!" said Jasper. "I can't believe it either!" He flopped down in the uncomfortable visitor chair. "We were perfect together!"

Call wished he could reach Jasper so he could strangle him. "No, I meant I can't believe you went through six checkpoints and a potentially embarrassing full-body search just so you could come here and complain about your love life!"

"You're the only one I can talk to, Call," said Jasper.

"You mean because I'm chained to this floor and can't get away?"

"Exactly." Jasper seemed pleased. "Everyone else bolts when they see me. But they don't understand. I have to get Celia back."

"Jasper," said Call. "Tell me something, and please answer honestly."

Jasper nodded.

"Is this the Assembly's new strategy for torturing me until I give them information?"

Just as he spoke, a thin tendril of smoke rose from the ground-floor level, followed by the flicker of flames. In the distance, an alarm started to sound.

The Panopticon was on fire.

CHAPTER TWO

THE TWO GUARDS who had brought Jasper to Call's cell began talking to each other in hushed tones. From the other side of the prison, some shouting began and then abruptly ceased.

"I think I better go." Jasper rose to his feet, looking around anxiously.

"No!" one of the guards barked. "This is an emergency. No visitors moving around on their own. For your safety, you're going to have to follow us while we escort the prisoner to an evacuation vehicle."

"You want me next to the Enemy of Death when he's outside his cell?" Jasper demanded, as though he had something to be worried about. "How is *that* safe?"

Call rolled his eyes.

One of the guards deactivated a section of the elemental wall and entered Call's cell, putting a fresh set of cuffs on him.

"Come on," the guard said. "You walk between us and the apprentice goes in front."

Call dug in his heels. "Something's wrong," he said.

"The place is on fire," Jasper said, looking behind him. "I'd say something's wrong."

Call went on. "I've been listening to a panel of mages tell me how invulnerable this place is for weeks. How nothing can break into it or destroy it. It shouldn't be on fire."

The guards were looking increasingly nervous. "Quiet down and come on," said one, hauling Call out of his cell by the arm.

"'*Fire wants to burn*,'" said Jasper, looking intently at Call. He was quoting the Cinquain, the five lines of text that described elemental magic. The guards gave him a look. They must have remembered it from school.

The air was getting hotter outside Call's cell. People were running in the hallways now, and yelling. All the other cells had been emptied of their inhabitants, prisoners marching in lines toward the exits.

"I know that," Call said. "But this place shouldn't burn."

"We've been warned about your silver tongue," said the guard, shoving Call ahead of him. "Shut up and move."

Chunks of melting rock and metal were starting to fall from the roof. At that point, Call decided to stop worrying about why this was happening and began to worry about making it out alive. Call, Jasper, and the two guards hurried along the corridor, which was getting hotter and hotter. Call stumbled along, his bad leg sending shooting pains through him. He hadn't walked this much in months.

There was a crash. Up ahead part of the floor was disintegrating in a fountain of burning cinders and chunks of fiery stone. Call stared, knowing he was right — this was no normal fire.

He just hoped he was going to be around to say *I told you so.*

The guards who'd been holding him let go. For a moment Call thought they were going to try an alternate path through the prison, but instead they bolted ahead, almost knocking over Jasper. They jumped across the collapsing floor just as it gave way entirely, landing safely on the other side. They got up and dusted themselves off.

"Hey!" Jasper yelled, looking incredulous. "You can't just leave us here!"

One of the guards looked ashamed. The other just glared. "My parents died in the Cold Massacre," he said. "As far as I'm concerned, you can burn to death, Constantine Madden."

Call flinched back.

"But what about me?" Jasper shouted as they walked away. "I'm not the Enemy of Death!"

But they had disappeared. Jasper whirled around, coughing. He looked accusingly at Call.

"This is all your fault," he said.

"Good to see you facing death bravely, Jasper," said Call. The upside of Jasper being here, he thought, was that Jasper never made him feel guilty, even when he probably should. It was impossible not to believe that Jasper deserved everything that happened to him.

"Use your chaos magic!" Jasper coughed. The air was thick and full of smoke and soot. "Devour the walls or the fire or something!"

Call held his hands out. His wrists were chained. A mage at his level couldn't do magic without his hands.

Jasper muttered a rude word and spun away, throwing his right arm out straight. The air in front of him seemed to vibrate and then solidify. A bridge over the collapsed part of the floor hung shimmering in the air.

Call didn't pause to marvel over the fact Jasper had actually done something useful — and not just useful, but actually impressive. He ran as fast as his leg could carry him, reserving the right to be amazed later.

Neither Call nor Jasper were that sure of the way out, but the fire had narrowed their choices. They bolted down the way open to them. Call gritted his teeth against the pain and tried his hardest not to stumble. The air was hot enough that even opening his mouth to speak hurt.

They came to a propped-open door that looked heavy and magical and almost impossible to get through in time if it had been closed. With relief, they scrambled through. Jasper knocked away the blockage, slamming the door behind them and buying them a little relief from the heat and the smoke.

Call panted, hands on his knees. They seemed be in one of the back passageways of the Panopticon. He could smell bleach and laundry detergent, all mixed up with smoke and burning. Corridors snaked off in all directions and there were no windows. A massive pillar of fire had suddenly formed in the corridor just ahead of them.

Jasper stumbled back, letting out a cry.

They were done for. They were going to be burned up, trapped in the hall between blazes. Call remembered navigating the fire maze of the year before, how he drew on chaos to take all the air out of the room — a desperate act that worked to put out the fire, but took all the air they needed to breathe along with it. Without Aaron's intervention, they would have died.

Call wished for his magic right then, wished for it despite remembering how he'd misused it.

Fire wants to burn. Water wants to flow. Air wants to rise. Earth wants to bind. Chaos wants to devour.

And the line of the Cinquain he'd added, just to be funny: *Call wants to live.*

The line haunted him. He pulled against his bonds, but they were as firm as ever, his magic out of reach. The fire ahead of them unwound like a snake, growing taller and taller, fire spreading from its upper part like the unfolding hood of a cobra.

Then a face formed in the fire — a familiar face. A girl's face, made entirely out of flames.

"Makar," said Tamara's sister, Ravan. She had been consumed by the element of fire, and lived on as a Devoured of fire, an elemental with a person's soul. Or a person with an element's soul. Call had once broken into a prison of elementals with Aaron and Tamara, and had seen the Devoured of Air and Fire and Earth and Water there. As far as he knew, there had never been a Devoured of chaos. The idea was terrifying.

"This is no time for dawdling," Ravan instructed. "Through the third doors on the right, you will find the way outside."

Her face vanished, bleeding into the flames. The fire changed shape, becoming a sparking, flaming archway.

"What. Is. That?" Jasper demanded.

"A fire elemental," Call said, not wanting to implicate Tamara when he had no idea what was going on. "I know her. She lives at the Magisterium."

"So this is a jailbreak? You made me part of your stupid jailbreak?" Jasper shouted, voice cracking. "This really *is* all your fault, Call. I —"

"Shut up, Jasper," Call said, pushing Jasper toward the third door. "You can yell at me when we're outside the burning building."

"Once again swept along by the cruel broom of fate," Jasper muttered as they went.

As Ravan had instructed, they bolted down the hallway and then turned right at two double doors with a long wooden bar laid across them. Jasper grabbed the bar and yanked it to the side. Call threw himself against the doors, and they burst open.

Sunlight and air. Jasper flung himself out the doors and then yelled. There was a thumping noise. "Stairs!" he shouted. "Watch out for the stairs."

Behind Call, everything was flames. He took a deep breath and followed Jasper outside. There *were* steps, a short flight down, with Jasper at the bottom, rubbing his knee. But there was also sunlight and fresh air and clouds and all the things that Call hadn't seen in so long. He sucked in a greedy breath and then another.

"Come on," Jasper said. "Before someone sees you."

As they moved away from the prison, the smoke thinned. Call looked back.

The Panopticon was a huge gray stone circle behind them, shaped like an upside-down bucket. Orange flames leaped from the windows and roof.

They came to a stretch of green lawn. There'd been no window in Call's room, but if there had, this is what he would have been able to see: flat greenness, a fence in the distance, and trees beyond that.

Right now it was a scene of total chaos. Groups of prisoners were chained together, guards circling them. Others were being loaded into vans. Mages in olive green Assembly robes were running over the grass, waving their arms, trying to direct panicked, soot-blackened guards, officers, and prisoners in different directions.

One of the Assembly Members caught sight of Call and shouted for guards.

"Where's my ride?" said Jasper, coughing. "I gotta get out of here."

"You're just going to *leave* me?" Call said.

"I know what happens if I hang around you," Jasper replied. "I'll get dragged into some horror show, with severed heads and Chaos-ridden. No, thank you. I have to win Celia back. I don't want to die."

"At least take these off me." Call held out his chained wrists. "Give me a chance, Jasper."

Guards were making their way toward Call now, talking to one another as though they were planning strategy. They weren't moving fast though and with Call's back turned they couldn't see what Jasper was about to do.

"Fine," he said, and edged over to grab Call's wrists. "Wait — what are these *made* of? I've never seen metal like this."

"You two," a voice barked. Call practically jumped out of his skin. It was an Assembly member in a white suit — *Anastasia Tarquin*, he realized in a paralyzing moment of mixed relief and fear. Her silver hair was pulled tightly back and her pale eyes blazed. "Get over here. Now, now." She snapped her fingers, her gaze sweeping over Call impersonally, as if she didn't know him at all. "Hurry up."

The guards stopped advancing, looking relieved that someone else was taking over.

Muttering imprecations, Jasper fell in beside Call and let

Anastasia lead them across the grass. "Transporting the Makar," she said, holding up her hand every time someone seemed to be about to approach or question them. "We have to get him moved as quickly as possible. Out of my way!"

A beige van was parked at the far end of the grass. Anastasia opened the back doors and hustled Call in. He couldn't see the driver up front.

Jasper balked. "There's really no reason for me to go in a car with prisoners —"

"You're a witness," Anastasia snapped. "Get in there, deWinter, or I'll tell your parents you didn't cooperate with the Assembly."

Eyes wide, Jasper scrambled in behind Call. The van had benches along both sides and bars above head level that cuffs could be slotted into to keep the prisoners in place. Call took a seat, and Jasper went to a place on the opposite side. No one affixed Call's handcuffs. Instead, the doors slammed shut, plunging them into cool darkness.

"This is weird," Call said.

"I am registering a complaint," Jasper replied in a subdued voice. "With someone. Someone will hear about this."

The van lurched forward, taking a few turns and then speeding up on what seemed to be a highway. Call couldn't guess where they were going. He wasn't even entirely sure of the location of the Panopticon in the first place, much less where they might take prisoners in case of a problem.

He puzzled over the presence of Anastasia and Ravan.

Anastasia had told him that she was Constantine Madden's mother, and that since Call had Constantine's soul, she would help him. Anastasia had been in charge of the elementals at the Magisterium. She could have engineered all of this. But if she had, what would she do next? The whole Assembly would be looking for Call. She couldn't just take him to some remote place until things blew over. The whole Enemy of Death thing was never going to blow over.

He went over Anastasia's involvement, the probability of this being a jailbreak, his fear of never seeing his dad again, his worry that Master Rufus would once again believe Call had been lying to him, and his concern that if they lurched around another curve he was going to get carsick again and again, with no new conclusions, so it was with a heavy heart that he felt the van stop. The back doors opened and light flooded in, making Call blink against it.

The driver stood in front of the open doors. She took off her newsboy cap. Long dark braids tumbled over her shoulders and a familiar grin lit her face. Call's heart flipped over in his chest.

Tamara.

CHAPTER THREE

CALL STARED AT Tamara, absolutely stunned. She looked different. Or maybe she didn't — maybe his memory of her had faded over six months. But he didn't think so. He'd thought about her so much he couldn't imagine he'd forgotten anything about her. Not that it mattered — did it matter? He realized he was still staring and that Tamara was probably expecting him to say something. He was saved by Havoc, who leaped into the van with a loud bark and began licking Call's face with vigor.

"Jasper," Tamara said, frowning at the other occupant of the van. "What are you doing here?"

"Have you lost your mind? You organized a jailbreak?" Jasper demanded, sputtering with rage. "And you didn't even tell me so that I could visit *on another day?*"

"Sorry I didn't check on your social plans." She rolled her eyes, climbing into the van. Pushing Havoc off Call, her fingers going to the wolf's ruff in a friendly gesture. . . .

Call couldn't speak. He had so much to say that it got tangled between the thinking of it and the saying it out loud. He was so happy just to be looking at Tamara, so happy that she still liked him enough to be helping him. And yet he knew there weren't any apologies big enough for him to give her.

She looked at him and smiled softly. "Hi, Call."

He felt as if he could barely swallow. Her face had changed subtly in the past half year, but up close she looked less different than he'd thought. She still had the same big, dark, sympathetic eyes. He spoke hoarsely: "Tamara. Did you — plan all this?"

"Not without help," she said, ushering Call out of the van. He jumped down beside her, stretching his aching leg.

They were standing in front of a pretty cottage in the center of a clearing. A little lake was off to the side, with a bridge going over it. Standing in front of the house was Anastasia Tarquin, her white car parked in the driveway.

Anastasia was still wearing her white suit, now marked with soot. She gazed at Call in that way that made him incredibly nervous, as if he were watching a mother lion prowling toward him across the savanna.

"I'll stay in the van," Jasper said breathlessly. "Later you can drop me somewhere. Like a gas station, anything. I'll get back on my own."

"Anastasia helped me," Tamara said, mostly to Call. "She

let me go down to talk to Ravan." She looked at her feet. "I didn't have too many other people to talk to, after Aaron died and you were . . . gone."

"You could have talked to me," said Jasper, still in the van.

"You just wanted to talk about Celia," said Tamara. "And nobody would talk to me about Call because —"

"Because they think I'm the Enemy of Death," Call said. "And that I wanted Aaron dead."

"They don't all think that," said Tamara in a small voice. "But most of them, yeah."

"Call, Tamara," Anastasia directed from the porch, "come inside." She narrowed her eyes. "You, too, Jasper."

Grumbling, Jasper finally hopped out of the prison van.

"When did you learn to drive?" Call asked Tamara.

"Kimiya taught me," Tamara answered as they went up the front steps. "I told her I needed to be distracted from — you know. Thinking about you and Aaron."

You and Aaron. Aaron had died and Call had lived but it must have seemed like a sort of living death to Tamara, Call trapped in the Panopticon and everyone else believing he was evil.

He realized how terrified he'd been that Tamara would believe the same thing about him. He felt almost weak with relief that apparently she didn't.

Inside, the house had a pretty living room, with lace curtains and small tables covered in doilies. There was a pitcher of lemonade on a coffee table. It was welcoming, but the way a candy-covered witch's house was welcoming. Still, he wasn't going to complain. He wasn't in jail and Tamara was here. They'd even brought Havoc.

"Let me see those cuffs," Tamara said as Call sat down on the first couch he'd encountered in months. Who would have thought you could miss couches? Tamara frowned. "What are these made out of? It isn't metal."

"You can't remove them without special tools," Anastasia informed her. "Unfortunately, I don't have those here." She stood up. "Call, come with me. I'll see if I can improvise something."

Not knowing how long he had with Tamara, he was reluctant to give up any time with her, but the cuffs did need to come off. Reluctantly, he stood and followed Anastasia into the kitchen.

She pointed to a stool. There was a big, heavy black bag on the counter, like an old-fashioned doctor's tool kit. Reaching inside, she brought out a few crystals, which she set on a tray. Then she turned on the burner beneath them.

As they heated, she turned toward Call. "It was unfortunate we couldn't get to you sooner," she said. "I know it was hard on you, waiting."

Call shifted in his seat. Anastasia acted like she knew what Call was thinking or feeling a lot. Sometimes she was right, sometimes she wasn't, but her conviction never wavered.

She had another conviction, too, one she'd mentioned to him the only time she'd ever visited him in the Panopticon. She believed that since she was Constantine Madden's mother, she was Call's mother, too.

Call didn't think it worked that way. But he knew better than to argue with Anastasia. She seemed absolutely sure of herself. He'd decided to just never mention it again and hope it wouldn't come up.

"Tamara, of course, was devastated not to be able to visit you," she added.

Call wanted to believe that was true. "She's a good friend."

"Friend?" Anastasia laughed a tinkling laugh. "She has such a crush on you. I think it's sweet."

Call stared at Anastasia, his mind reeling. Tamara didn't have a crush on him! That was ridiculous. Tamara was beautiful and smart and rich and had perfect eyebrows.

As long as he'd known Tamara, he'd known he was out of her league. He remembered watching her dancing with Aaron at the beginning of his Copper Year. They'd looked good together. He'd known he would never look good with Tamara. If they danced together — even if he could keep up with the way his leg was — he was sure he'd step on her feet.

The crystals started making an odd keening noise and Anastasia turned off the stove. "Earth and fire together," she explained. "Easier to draw on this way. "

Then with one hand she reached out and *melted* the chain connecting the cuffs. Call had to shift abruptly to avoid getting splashed with liquid metal. It hit the linoleum and smoked ominously, the plastic blackening around the spatters.

Anastasia frowned at the floor. "This is all I can do for

now, but it should give you greater movement until we remove the cuffs themselves."

Call was barely paying attention. He was staring at the melting floor and wondering: Could it be true? Could Tamara really like him? Anastasia was kind of weird and maybe a little crazy. She probably didn't know what she was talking about.

But what if she did?

"Go on back to the living room," Anastasia told him. "I'll be along in a moment, after I clean things up."

Mechanically, Call returned to where Tamara and Jasper were discussing the house.

"Anastasia found us this safe house where we can hide out from the mages," Tamara was saying. "She put disruptive air magic around it to keep it from being found. We can hide out and make our next plans."

Call stared at her as though she wasn't one of his best friends. As though he hadn't shared a common room with her for the past three years. No, Tamara couldn't like him. If anything, she'd liked Aaron. "How long before you have to go back to the Magisterium?" he blurted out. "I mean, they're going to notice you're gone."

Great, he thought. *It sounds like I want to get rid of her.* He had the horrifying thought that he might be as tongue-tied around Tamara as he'd been around Celia after he found out she wanted to go on a date with him. What if he ruined their friendship? What if he made a fool of himself?

Tamara didn't meet his eyes. "I can't go back, Call."

"What about *me*?" Jasper yelled. "What about me going back to school? I have to go! Celia is there!"

Call couldn't quite process the sacrifice Tamara was planning to make.

"Ever?" Call asked her. "You can't go back to school ever?"

Maybe he did have devastating charm after all. Maybe she really did like him. Or maybe she was a really great friend.

Maybe he was never going to know.

Tamara gave Call a long look. "I'm not going to sit around learning magic while apprentices are talking about the mages catching you and chopping off your head. I'm not going back unless you're coming with me. And to do that, we're going to have to clear your name."

Call swallowed hard. He knew the other students would say terrible things about him, but he hadn't thought about the whole head-chopping part. Worse, he didn't think there *was* a way to clear his name — not as long as everyone thought it was secretly *Constantine Madden*.

"Are you listening to yourselves?" Jasper demanded. "How do you plan on doing that?"

"I don't know yet," Tamara admitted. "But Ravan helped before and she'll help with this."

"*Ravan?*" Jasper said. "That was *Ravan* back at the Panopticon? Tamara, you can't trust one of the Devoured, even if she was once your sister!"

Call's mind was whirling, still thinking of what Tamara had done by breaking him out of prison. And with Anastasia Tarquin, of all people. How had Tamara and Anastasia wound up working together? What did Anastasia want?

As Jasper and Tamara kept on bickering, Call found himself staring at Tamara, memorizing her — her eyes, her tone of voice when she was annoyed, the slant of her mouth as she smiled. He was afraid he was going to lose her again. He was used to them being in trouble and having an unlikely scheme for getting out of it. He was used to them dragging an unwilling Jasper into that scheme. But before, Aaron had always been with them.

He'd always kind of assumed that everyone went along with Aaron, and since Aaron liked Call, they put up with Call, too.

Without Aaron, everything felt strange and wrong. Unbalanced. Uncertain.

Without Aaron, would Tamara still like him? Could they still be friends when there were just two of them, not three?

The thought of Aaron closed, like a cold fist around Call's heart. Aaron ought to be here, bickering about what they were all going to do. Instead, he was gone. Call and Tamara had been left behind together. The thought made Call's heart pound, with nerves and more.

Anastasia Tarquin came back into the room. Trailing behind her was a familiar figure in heavy robes. Tamara gasped and half rose from the couch.

It was Master Joseph.

Call started up from the couch, ready to attack, but no Chaos curled from his fingers. Even without the chain, the cuffs somehow prevented him from using any magic.

Tamara gasped. Jasper backed up a few steps and then froze, staring. Of course, the last time he'd seen Constantine's teacher, the tomb of the Enemy of Death had been collapsing around them.

"What," said Jasper in a strangled voice, "is *he* doing here?"

"Anastasia?" Tamara demanded, her voice rising. "What's going on?"

"I'm afraid I wasn't entirely honest with you," Anastasia said. "Neither about myself nor about my reasons for freeing Call. You see, before I was called Anastasia Tarquin, I had another name: Eliza Madden. I was Constantine and Jericho Madden's mother."

Call's heart sank.

Tamara's eyes were huge. "*What?*"

"Yes," Anastasia said. "I am sure you never thought of the Enemy of Death as having a mother, but he does. I lost both my sons, but I won't lose Call. I am not going to let the mages lock him up to rot. And I am certainly not going to let them put him to death after some show trial."

"Put me to . . . *death?*" Call echoed. Was that her fear talking or did she know something? Was that true?

"We were going to clear his name! Instead, you're going to put him back in the hands of the monster responsible for you losing your sons in the first place?" Tamara demanded, gesturing at Master Joseph.

"That's a lie," Master Joseph said. Then he flicked his hand and sent Tamara flying back against the couch. Her body bounced against the cushions.

"You leave her alone!" Call shouted, everything else forgotten. Havoc began to growl, and fire sparked at the center of Jasper's palm.

Master Joseph took in the sight of them pityingly. "I had hoped you might come willingly, but I am entirely capable of bringing you by force."

Anastasia's face was like marble. "You will not hurt Callum," she said. "Joseph!"

She couldn't really trust Master Joseph, could she? Call tried to stand but was knocked down by another wave from Master Joseph's hand. Master Joseph moved his wrist, twisting it, and a vortex of wind rose from his fingers and spun toward them.

Call and Tamara were flattened against the sofa, Jasper pinned to the wall. Even Havoc was knocked to the ground, whimpering and growling over the rush of the wind.

The door flew open behind Master Joseph. Through it marched the Chaos-ridden — the mindless, zombielike followers of the Enemy of Death. Making them had been one of Constantine's greatest crimes — and also, according to people like Master Joseph, his greatest achievement.

Implacably, the Chaos-ridden surrounded Call, Tamara,

and Jasper, seizing them by the arms and marching them outside. Once they got that far, they stopped, forming a loose circle. They seemed totally bizarre and out of place in the pretty clearing with the neat little house at the center.

Anastasia and Master Joseph had come out onto the porch. Anastasia was watching Call with the same vast hunger as before. Another car gleamed in the driveway. Havoc, barking and snarling, ran around the circle, unable to approach.

Why had the Chaos-ridden stopped? Call knew they didn't make their own decisions; they were the shells of human beings who had had chaos forced into their souls, and were totally obedient to their Master.

Their Master. Constantine Madden had made the Chaos-ridden. He was the Makar, their Master. It was the one sort of good thing about having Constantine's soul.

Call cleared his throat. This was going to be embarrassing.

"Release me," he said. "I am your Master. I am the Enemy of Death. His soul is like mine. Release me, Chaos-ridden."

The last two times he'd done this, it had worked.

This time, nothing happened.

It felt like Call was slamming into a wall. The Chaos-ridden just stared at him, their coruscating eyes, like Havoc's, whirling.

Maybe it was because of the cuffs, he thought, trying to contort his hands to push them off his wrists.

Then the door of the new car opened. Out stepped a tall

boy with tousled brown hair. He wore a leather jacket and a nasty smirk.

Alex Strike. Aaron's murderer, and the only other chaos mage Call knew of.

A growl tore out of Call's throat as he lunged toward Alex. Behind him, Tamara was screaming and kicking at the Chaos-ridden who were holding her.

"I'll kill you!" There were tears on Call's face as he flung himself at Alex. "I'll kill you!"

"Stop him," said Alex lazily. Seconds later, Call felt himself seized by a dozen Chaos-ridden, their grips like iron.

Alex's eyes danced. "I made these," he said, gesturing toward the Chaos-ridden in the clearing. "I am their Makar — not you, not Constantine. They obey *me*."

"That's enough," Anastasia said from the porch. "You are not to harm Call. *No one* is to harm Call. Alex, do you understand? We need to put our differences behind us."

Alex looked toward her sharply, then at Master Joseph as though he hoped to hear something different.

Instead, Master Joseph smiled at all of them, like everything was going perfectly well. "Yes, no one is to harm anyone else. Let's all go back to the stronghold peaceably. We have much to discuss. The future we have long awaited is finally here."

Alex's face turned petulant, but neither of the adults seemed to notice.

Anastasia's eyes were fixed on Call. "I know you're probably feeling very vexed with me right now, but I know what's best for you. You need protection. The mages only understand shows of strength. You threw yourself on their mercy and see what it got you?"

"Ravan will know!" Tamara yelled. "When I don't meet her like I said I would, she'll know you betrayed us. She'll tell someone."

Anastasia shook her head and clucked her tongue as though Tamara had been slow in class. "Who will believe her? She's an escaped elemental who burned down a prison."

Tamara looked defeated and furious with herself. Call wanted to tell Tamara that it wasn't her fault that this plan was going sideways, that this kind of thing seemed to always happen when he was around. But before he could say anything, the dead thing holding him began to drag him back to the van. In a few moments, they were loaded inside, along with Havoc.

"Seriously?" Jasper said glumly from one of the benches. "Clandestine meetings with the Enemy of Death's minions are definitely not going to clear your name, Call. This is the opposite, in fact. This is the opposite of clearing your name."

"Nobody planned this, Jasper!" Tamara snapped.

"Master Joseph did," Jasper said, jarringly accurate. Call was used to snarky comments, but this was different. Jasper was right.

Havoc howled in frustration and paced the small space before settling against Call's leg.

Call expected to hear the engine start and someone get into the front, but instead he felt the whole van lift unsteadily into the air. They all tumbled sideways, yelling. Jasper knocked into Call before sprawling over Havoc. Call banged his bad leg hard against the bench. Tamara toppled into him, getting her hair in his mouth and her knee in a place Call didn't want to think about.

Ow.

Then the van lurched again and they rolled in the opposite direction.

"Hey!" Call shouted when he got his breath back. "I thought no one was supposed to get hurt!"

After a few more minutes of lurching, the van steadied and moved more gently through the air. They stayed on the floor until they were sure it was safe and then gingerly got back on the benches.

Jasper rubbed his neck.

Tamara was quiet beside Call. Taking a deep breath, he nervously reached out with his cuffed hands and took one of hers. It was warm and soft and he held it tightly as they flew toward the stronghold that had once belonged to the real Enemy of Death.

CHAPTER FOUR

HOURS PASSED, DURING which Call dozed on and off. He was keyed up but also exhausted. He kept thinking of Alastair — how would his dad know where he was? He'd know Call had escaped from prison. Pretty soon everyone in the mage world would know there was a Makar on the loose. Call thought of his dad being worried and felt hollow inside.

Tamara didn't sleep. Every time Call opened his eyes he saw her staring miserably into the dark. Once, tears were sliding down her face. He wondered if she was upset because the jailbreak hadn't worked. Or maybe she was missing Aaron.

Tamara had saved Call's life when Alex Strike had been trying to steal his chaos magic. But in saving Call's life, she had doomed Aaron. Aaron, the nicest and best guy Call had ever known.

She could have saved either one of them and she had chosen Call. No one in their right mind would choose Call.

He didn't wonder if she regretted it. He wondered how *much* she regretted it. Or at least he had, until Anastasia's words.

Now he didn't know what to think. On the one hand, he wanted to believe it. On the other hand, the source was Anastasia and she wasn't exactly reliable.

The van finally thumped to the ground in a landing that tossed them all onto the floor. The back doors were flung open by Alex Strike. Call felt his flesh crawl again at the sight of Alex and wondered if he'd ever get used to seeing him. Ever not feel the urge to make Alex's head swell and pop like an overripe berry.

He didn't want to get used to it.

"Welcome home," Alex said, stepping back so they could pile out of the van. He wasn't alone — there was a half circle of Chaos-ridden behind him. Master Joseph was nowhere to be seen.

Overhead the sun was setting in a blaze of red and purple. They were on an island, in the middle of a wide river — banks were visible on either side in the distance. Wild grass grew uncut among lilac trees.

In front of the vans rose a massive house of yellow stone with towers, like those of a castle. There was a huge porticoed entrance. It put even Tamara's family home to shame in terms of size, although the weeds around it were overgrown and the place itself looked both long abandoned and a little weird.

Havoc, freed from the confines of the van, barked loudly. Call was about to shush him when a chorus of barks and howls answered.

Tamara's eyes widened. "Other Chaos-ridden wolves," she said as the noise went on. It was beautiful and eerie. Havoc seemed not to know what to do with himself — he lunged forward curiously before cringing back against Call's leg. Call stroked his head.

Alex laughed. "Stupid animal."

Tamara bristled. "Don't talk about Havoc that way."

"Who says I was talking about Havoc?" Alex started up the stairs toward the front door of the house. The Chaos-ridden started to move as well, herding Call, Jasper, and Tamara toward the entrance to the house.

They went through the big front doors, into a massive entryway. A huge stained-glass chandelier hung from a roof, lost in shadows overhead. A wide stairway climbed the inside of the entryway, leading to who-knew-how-many floors. Over a fireplace, Constantine Madden's silver mask hung — the very mask that Master Joseph had been wearing the first time Call had seen him, the mask that had allowed Master Joseph to play the part of Constantine for so long while he'd waited for Call to grow up and take Constantine's place.

Above it hung the Alkahest, air shimmering around it to

indicate some kind of magical defense. Once created to destroy a Chaos-user, Alex had somehow modified it to steal Chaos. He'd used it to kill Aaron and steal his power. If it wasn't for the Alkahest, there would be no band of Chaos-ridden obeying Alex. If it wasn't for the Alkahest, Aaron wouldn't be dead.

Jasper made an impressed noise. Tamara glared at him.

"Yes, it's a nice little cottage," said Alex airily. "Come along. You" — he flicked his fingers toward the Chaos-ridden — "can stay here."

Call and his companions trailed after Alex into a big room with a farmhouse table running down the center. Master Joseph was there, stirring the contents of an enormous cauldron with a heavy metal spoon.

"Ah," he said. "Glad to see you made it. See, everything is very civilized here. This isn't like the prison you came from."

But it's a prison all the same, Call thought. Still, he let Master Joseph speak a few words over his cuffs and pull them off his wrists. He rubbed the skin underneath self-consciously.

"Where's Anastasia?" he asked. She made him uncomfortable, but he did believe she was looking out for his well-being.

"Upstairs, getting ready for dinner," said Master Joseph. He indicated the contents of the pot.

"Eye-of-newt?" Call guessed. "Toe-of-frog stew?"

"My famous five-alarm chili, actually," said Master Joseph. "Drew always loved it."

At the mention of Master Joseph's dead son, Call froze. Master Joseph had said he didn't blame Call for Drew's death, even though he'd been at least partially responsible for it. Call was sure that part of Master Joseph hated him, and that hate might bubble up at any moment.

Master Joseph wanted Call to be Constantine Madden reborn. He wanted the Enemy of Death. Callum Hunt, even with the same soul, was going to be a constant source of disappointment.

"What do you want me to do with Call and his backup band?" Alex asked in a bored voice.

"Call's and Tamara's rooms are in the Red Wing," said Master Joseph. "As for our unexpected guest . . ." He looked at Jasper. "Put him in Drew's old room."

"Oh no," said Jasper. "That seems creepy."

Master Joseph gave Jasper a smile that was half snarl. "We, those who nobly battle death, have been accused of being macabre before. Of being too comfortable with death. We don't like to give credence to that kind of talk. We simply refuse to acknowledge death as an end. That is all."

Jasper didn't look reassured.

"Besides, the bedrooms are the only place the Chaos-ridden don't go," Alex added.

"On the other hand," said Jasper, "that'll be fine."

He still glared at Call, though, as they went upstairs, and mouthed *It's all your fault* at him before he was escorted off to something called the Green Wing by a silent Chaos-ridden.

Call and Tamara were taken down a corridor where the walls were red. Tamara was shown to a room across the hall while Alex personally brought Call into his chamber, leaning across him to flick on the light.

"Anastasia decorated it," he said. "What do you think?"

At first the room seemed fine. It was normal, plain, with navy-and-white-striped sheets and pillows. There was a sofa and a desk. Only slowly did the horror of what he was looking at creep in. Family photos littered all the surfaces — Constantine Madden, laughing with his brother, Jericho. Waving over a railing with his parents. On a camping trip with the whole family.

Photos of Constantine by himself, getting awards at school, ceremonies where new stones were put into his wristband. Grinning in his Silver Year uniform. Candid photos of him with his friends were shoved into the frames of the mirrors, tacked above the bed.

Friends that were now mostly dead, murdered in the Third Mage war.

"All the books are Constantine's favorite books," said Alex in a gloating voice. "All the clothes in the wardrobe are the clothes he wore when he was your age. They're hoping it's going to trigger some flood of memories, but I don't think it's going to work."

"Go away," said Call. Next to him, Havoc was whining uneasily. He could sense Call was upset but didn't know why.

Alex leaned against the doorjamb. "But this is so funny."

Call remembered when he'd admired Alex. He'd thought Alex was just Master Rufus's assistant, a cool older apprentice who had been kind to Call. But all that kindness had been fake. Everything about Alex was fake, like the illusion magic he'd favored.

"I'm about to change for dinner," said Call. "Get out or watch me strip — it's your choice."

Alex rolled his eyes and disappeared, slamming the door behind him.

Call went over to examine the photos shoved into the mirror frame. Most of them were of Constantine with his friends. He recognized a much younger Alastair Hunt, his arm around Constantine, grinning and pointing off at something in the distance. And there was Call's mom, Sarah, looking so young with loose hair and a pretty smile. She stood next to Constantine with something strapped to her hip.

Miri. The knife she'd made. She was wearing Miri. Call felt the back of his throat start to ache as he remembered she'd used that knife to carve words into the wall of the ice cave where she died.

KILL THE CHILD.

Call wandered over to the wardrobe and yanked open the doors.

The clothes inside probably would have been more disturbing to someone who hadn't grown up with Alastair Hunt and therefore shopped in a lot of thrift stores and vintage emporiums. Lots of black jeans with rips in the knee and long cargo shorts. Beside them, thermal waffle shirts, white tees, and a lot of flannel. There was also a beat-up jean jacket. The '90s had returned and were living here in Call's closet.

Despite what Alex had said, Call hoped Master Joseph had actually bought this stuff secondhand. That would have been creepy enough, but as he inspected the jean jacket, which had patches and writing on it, he came to the much creepier conclusion — all this stuff really had once belonged to Constantine Madden.

Call really hoped the underwear was new. He did not want to wear the Underoos of an Evil Overlord.

The door opened and Jasper came in.

"I c-c-can't," he sputtered. "I can't stay in there!"

"What now?" Call demanded, sick of Jasper's complaints. After all, none of them had wanted to be kidnapped. None of them wanted to sleep here. "It can't be creepier than this!"

Jasper looked around the room, taking it in. Then he turned back to Call. "Come with me." There was grimness in his voice that made Call trail after him, Havoc on his heels.

They went down the red hall and into a green one, past two doors to another, which Jasper pushed open.

It was a big room with a large window. The light streaming in caught on cobwebs around the room. Dust had settled on most surfaces. It looked like no one had been in there since Drew had died. It was creepy, Call had to admit — especially with all the horses.

Horses on shelves lining an entire wall, arranged in the plastic hundreds. Horses on posters. Horses on a beside table lamp. Horses running on the sheets.

"That's a lot of . . ." Call managed, staring.

"You see?" Jasper said. "I can't sleep in here!"

Even Havoc looked a bit daunted. He sniffed the air worriedly.

"I guess the whole pony obsession wasn't just part of Drew's cover," Call said. He had to admit, this room might actually be worse than his.

"They watch me," Jasper said, already haunted. "No matter where I go in the room, they're watching me with their beady black eyes. It's horrible."

Tamara came into the room. Behind her, in the red hallway, a door was slightly ajar. "What are you looking at . . . whoa!" She blinked at the horses.

"What's your room like?" Jasper wanted to know.

"Not important," Tamara said, too quickly. "Totally boring."

Call narrowed his eyes at her, suspicious.

"Maybe I can sleep in there?" Jasper seemed delighted by the thought, as though what was wrong with their situation was the accommodations. He headed to the slightly ajar door in the red hall.

"You can't!" she said, trailing after him. "And there's no reason to look —"

But by then he'd jerked the door the rest of the way open.

For a moment, Call thought Jasper's face had grown flushed, but it was just a reflection of the inside of the room. It was pink. Really, really, really pink.

Tamara let out a long sigh. "I know we have bigger problems, but my room is embarrassing!"

The walls were painted a soft pink. The dark pink canopy bed was hung with gauzy, iridescent material. The bedding was neon pink and covered in ruffles. On top of it sat a massive stuffed unicorn with a silver cloth horn. On the floor rested a fuzzy pink rug in the shape of a heart.

"Wow," Call said.

"You should see the clothes in the closet," Tamara said. "No, actually, no one should ever see the clothes in the closet."

From down the stairs came a call. "Dinner!"

"Do you think this is some fiendish plot of Master Joseph's to make sure we don't get any sleep?" Call wanted to know as they trooped down the stairs. "Don't cults try to brainwash you by keeping you tired?"

Tamara wrinkled her nose like she was going to disagree, but didn't. Instead, she seemed to be weighing the possibility.

As they headed into the room with the long table, set for six and heaped with enough food to feed double that number, Call had to consider that Master Joseph might have a different fiendish scheme. In addition to keeping you sleep deprived, cults weren't supposed to feed you enough, but it seemed like Master Joseph was intent on feeding them way too much.

The cauldron of chili had been moved to the center of the table, where it bubbled deliciously, a mound of cheese atop it. More cheese was grated onto a plate, along with chopped green onions and a tub of sour cream. Golden squares of corn bread were stacked in the shape of a ziggurat beside a slab of butter with a knife sticking out of it and a jar of honey. On the nearby sideboard sat three pies — two pecan and one sweet potato. Call's stomach growled loudly enough for Jasper to turn in surprise, as though a Chaos-ridden wolf might be behind him.

A Chaos-ridden person slapped down a pitcher of what looked like sweet tea, hard enough to spill some, then looked at Call with an empty expression, tipped its head toward him in a kind of bow, and left the room. Call wondered at the violence with which the Chaos-ridden moved. He'd always thought they fought because they'd been commanded to, but maybe they had a bent toward murderousness.

Then he was too busy drooling to wonder about anything else.

Master Joseph looked pleased by their reactions. "Sit, sit. The others will be with us in a moment."

After many months in prison eating disgusting prison food, Call needed no urging. He slid into a seat and tucked the cloth napkin into his shirt eagerly.

"Do you think it might be poisoned?" Tamara whispered, sitting down beside him. Jasper sat on her other side, leaning in to hear what she was saying.

"He's going to eat it, too," said Call, cutting his gaze toward Master Joseph.

"He could have taken the antidote," Tamara insisted. "And given it to Alex and Anastasia."

"He wouldn't kidnap you and Call and give you customized bedrooms just to poison you," Jasper whispered back to them. "You're both idiots. The only person he would poison is me."

The doors opened and Anastasia came in, followed by Alex. Call had almost forgotten they knew each other well — Anastasia had married Alex's father in an attempt to conceal her identity as Eliza Madden. She looked regal in a white pantsuit, her hair drawn back in a smooth chignon. Alex had on jeans and a black shirt with a death's-head moth on the front. It was actually kind of cool, and Call found himself wishing he had one. (On the other hand, it *did* seem like the kind of thing an Evil Overlord might wear.)

Alex sat down and immediately started dishing himself up some chili. Once he was done, Jasper snatched the spoon from him and pretty soon everyone was digging into their food (except Anastasia, who took only some corn bread and nibbled on the edge).

At the first bite of chili, the flavors exploded in Call's mouth — sweet, spicy, smoky. It wasn't prison food, and it wasn't lichen. "The food of evil is so good," he muttered to Tamara, on his left.

"That's how they get you," she muttered back, but she was already on her second helping of corn bread.

"This is delightful," said Master Joseph, gazing around with a deceptively benign air. "I remember such meals with Constantine and his friends. Jasper, you make an excellent Alastair Hunt, and you, Tamara, of course would be Sarah."

Tamara looked horrified at the idea of being Call's mom. Call was just horrified by the whole conversation.

"Uh-huh," said Alex, looking like he was enjoying himself. "So who am I, then?"

"Not Jericho," said Anastasia flatly.

"You're Declan," said Master Joseph. "He was a nice boy."

Declan Novak had been Call's uncle. He'd died in the Cold Massacre, protecting Call's mother. Though he'd never met Declan, Call was sure he was nothing like Alex.

"I ought to be Constantine," Alex muttered. His gaze went to the other room, where the silver mask and the Alkahest hung over the fireplace.

"Wow," said Jasper loudly, breaking the uncomfortable silence that followed this pronouncement. "Who's ready for pie? I know I am."

He stood up with his plate, but Master Joseph gestured for him to stay where he was.

"Let Call choose the first piece of pie," said Master Joseph. "In this house, all things serve the Enemy of Death."

Alex banged his fork down. "So we're supposed to do whatever Call says just because he's got some dead guy's soul?"

"Yes," said Master Joseph, looking narrowly at Alex.

Jasper swallowed and sat down, pieless.

"Call doesn't even *want* it!" Alex burst out. "He doesn't care about making more Chaos-ridden! He doesn't want to lead an army against the Magisterium!"

"There is no Call," said Master Joseph. "There is only Constantine Madden. It's our job to make Callum Hunt understand who he is."

"That's not true," said Tamara, voice shaking. "Call is Call. Whatever made Constantine so messed up, it didn't happen to Call."

"What made Constantine so messed up, young lady," said Master Joseph, "was losing his best friend, his brother. His *counterweight*. Are you saying that hasn't happened to Call?"

At the mention of Aaron, Call saw red. He grabbed the dull knife from beside his plate and pointed it toward Alex. "I didn't *lose* my best friend. Alex murdered him. He *stole* his Makar power. But he'll never be half of what Aaron was."

Alex's eyes burned with fury. "I am twice any of you! I taught myself to modify the Alkahest and took the power of commanding chaos from another mage. I am the first Makar ever to have done that. I learned to create Chaos-ridden in mere months while you've *never* done it!"

Call thought of how his attempt at bringing back Jennifer Matsui had gone and said nothing.

"You're disgusting," Tamara said. "Being proud of that is *disgusting*."

"Both of you!" Master Joseph reprimanded. "*All* of you! I know it will be difficult to find common ground, but this isn't helping. You've accomplished many things, Alex, but all of them were built on the foundation of Constantine's discoveries. Let's give Call an opportunity to find who he is — if he doesn't, I will strip the power from him myself."

Call caught his breath, thinking of the Alkahest and what it could do. Master Joseph had spent years wishing for the power of chaos. Now he could have it, if he was willing to take it.

Jasper stood up and cut himself a large slice of pecan pie. Everyone stopped yelling and watched him as he put it on his own plate, sat down, and forked a big delicious-looking bite into his mouth.

"What?" he asked when he noticed them looking. "This *is* helping. Now they don't have to fight over who gets the first slice."

Alex looked like he might jump over the table and strangle Jasper. Call often felt the same way. But right then, Jasper's obnoxiousness seemed downright heroic.

Master Joseph sliced more pie, and Call ate an enormous piece of sweet potato and pecan, punctuating each bite with a vicious glare, trying to show dominance through superior pie eating. Alex's pie game was pathetic; he picked the nuts off the top of his pie and out of the middle, leaving the crust and the topping still on his plate. Call sneered at him.

Finally, Master Joseph stood up. "This has been a long day and it seems like it's time for rest. Call, there is ground hamburger meat for Havoc in the refrigerator. Help yourself to anything you need. I hope that you've realized the foolishness of trying to leave us. There are Chaos-ridden at every door to prevent your departure."

Call didn't say anything, since there was nothing to say. He was a prisoner again . . . and this time Jasper and Tamara were prisoners, too.

Anastasia left with a brief, uncomfortable squeeze of Call's shoulder and a kiss to the top of his head. He stayed still for it, trying not to wince. He'd never had a mother, but this wasn't what he thought it was supposed to be like.

Once they were alone at the top of the stairs, Tamara turned to Jasper and Call with a determined look and vowed in a harsh whisper, *"We're getting out of here."*

CHAPTER FIVE

THEY HELD THEIR meeting in the pink room, sprawled on the fuzzy, heart-shaped rug. As they strategized, Tamara savagely ripped lace from the hems and sleeves of some truly weird pastel-colored dresses. Pink was supposed to make people feel calmer, but all Call felt was depressed and very, very full.

"I can't believe your original escape plan requires *another* escape plan," Jasper said. "You suck at escaping."

Tamara fixed him with a glare. "I guess the more we escape, the better we'll get at it."

After a moment, Jasper brightened. "Maybe it's not *so* bad that we've been kidnapped. I mean, this is all very dramatic. When Celia understands what's happened to me, she's going to feel terrible for dumping me. She is going to hold my picture to her heart, fearing for my life and shedding a tear over the love we had. *If only he would come back*, she'll think, *I will beg him to be my boyfriend again!*"

Call goggled at Jasper, speechless.

"But, I mean, only if we don't escape too quickly," Jasper went on. "She needs time to find out I'm gone and work up to all that epic suffering. Maybe a few weeks. After all, the food is pretty good here."

"What if she has another boyfriend by then?" Tamara asked. "I mean —"

"Okay," Jasper said, cutting her off. "What are we going to do? It has to be tonight."

"I already checked the windows — at least the ones in this room. It's elemental stuff, like they use in the Panopticon," Tamara said. "It doesn't break. We might be able to get through it with magic, but it would take a lot of work and might trigger an alarm."

"So no going through a window," Jasper said. "What about getting a message to Ravan?"

Tamara shook her head. "To do that, we'd still have to get out of here. I could try to call up another fire elemental and send it to find her, but that's really advanced. I've never done anything like it."

"Well, Master Joseph did say that I was supposed to feed Havoc some stuff from the fridge, and he must know I'll have to walk him," Call said. "At least that will put us outside the building."

"We won't *all* be allowed to walk him," Tamara pointed out. "Master Joseph can't be that dumb."

Jasper frowned. "No. But there have to be other Chaos-ridden around, right? This is the stronghold of the Enemy of Death. This is where they all are."

"So?" Tamara asked, ripping another ruffle off a skirt, leaving a bunch of threads hanging down. "Isn't that even worse for us?"

Jasper slid a glance in Call's direction. "No, because it means there are some here that Call controls. What if we walk Havoc and then Call gets one of *his* Chaos-ridden to fight Alex's? It would be enough of a distraction to slip by them."

Call took a deep breath. "Maybe you two should run. You could take Havoc for a walk, just like you said, but then keep going. Havoc could help keep you safe from whatever's in the woods, and I could stay behind to try to stop them from following you. You could bring back help. The mage world might hate me, but they don't want me with Master Joseph — they'll think it's dangerous."

"Call, if we get away, Master Joseph is likely to leave here and take you with him," Tamara said. "He won't wait around for us to come back with the Assembly and an army. No, we've got to go together."

"Besides," said Jasper, "if the Assembly catches up with you and you're with Master Joseph, they'll assume you're there because you want to be."

Jasper, Call thought, had a rotten habit of being able to

always imagine the worst thing people might think. Probably because his mind worked that way, too. It didn't make him less right, though.

"Fine," Call said. "So what's the plan?"

Tamara took a deep breath. "The Chaos-ridden," she said.

"We get them to fight one another like I said?" Jasper looked delighted. "Really?"

"No," Tamara told him.

"Maybe all the ones in the house serve Alex," Call said.

"I don't think so," said Tamara. "Remember what he said: *I made these.* He couldn't have made all the Chaos-ridden in and around the house. There are just too many. Some of them must have been made by Constantine and be loyal to you."

Call remembered the Chaos-ridden servant in the dining room and the way it had bowed its head. "I think I know where to look," he said slowly.

The night air was cold, so they split up to get jackets and met back in the hallway outside their rooms. Jasper's sweater had a horse on it. Tamara was wearing a long pale green dress with the lace ripped off, and her jean jacket and newsboy cap. Call had Havoc beside him on a leash.

"Let's do this," Tamara said grimly.

They crept down the stairs and into the massive entryway. It was dark, the lights dimmed. Call handed Havoc's leash to Tamara and slipped into the dining room just as Master Joseph came down the stairs.

"What are you doing?" he demanded of Tamara and Jasper.

Call pressed his eye to the gap in the door. Master Joseph was wearing a fuzzy gray bathrobe, which ought to have been hilarious, but wasn't. There was a cruelty in his face that he had hidden at dinner.

"We need to walk Havoc," Tamara said, lifting her chin. "If we don't, bad things will happen. To your floor. And your carpets."

Havoc whined. Master Joseph sighed. "Very well," he said. "Stay in view of the house."

To Call's surprise, Master Joseph stood and watched as Tamara and Jasper opened the front door and — with incredulous looks at each other — stepped out onto the front porch. He could see water in the distance — the river that stood between them and the mainland. The house had what was probably considered a really good view, but Call was really starting to hate it.

Master Joseph stood for a moment as the door shut after them, then turned and walked off down the hall.

Call felt a little panicked as he turned around, facing the darkness of the dining room. Did Master Joseph care so little about Tamara and Jasper that he'd let them leave? Was he trying to show them they could trust him? Or was there something horrible outside that would keep them penned in — or even hurt them?

"Master," said a voice.

Call jumped. A shadow had loomed up out of the darkness. It was the Chaos-ridden who had bowed to him before.

He had dark hair and the coruscating eyes of all the Chaos-ridden. He limped when he walked. He must have been injured before he'd died. Sometimes it was hard for Call to remember the Chaos-ridden were all walking dead corpses. Call repressed a shudder at the thought that maybe it wasn't hard for other people.

"Take me outside," he said. "In a way Master Joseph won't notice."

"Yesss." The Chaos-ridden turned and led Call out of the dining room and down a series of turning passages. Call caught a glimpse of a huge room with a drain in the floor like a shower, and another room with shelf after shelf of glowing elementals trapped in jars. Call thought he even saw a room with shackles bolted to the walls.

Yikes.

The Chaos-ridden led him down a last corridor to a door that opened with the drawing of several rusty bolts. Beyond it was the side of the house and the massive overgrown lawn.

He'd made it.

Woods surrounded the stretch of grass, woods with unfamiliar trees. The air was cold, too, unseasonably cold for September. They must be up north. He headed toward the woods, hugging his arms around himself. He could worry about the chill later.

"Okay," Call said to the Chaos-ridden who had followed him, footfalls disturbingly silent. "I am going to wait here. Go to my friends — a girl in a hat, a wolf, and a boy with a weird haircut — and tell them where to find me. I mean, not with words. They won't understand you. But maybe you could point?"

The Chaos-ridden looked at him with his swirling eyes for a long moment. Call wondered if he should have described Tamara, Havoc, and Jasper a different way. Maybe the Chaos-ridden didn't understand which haircuts were weird. Maybe they had bad taste.

"Yesss," he said again. Although he did seem eerie, he also put Call's worries to rest. The Chaos-ridden lumbered off toward the front of the mansion.

Call sat down on a nearby log, looking back toward the huge house. Despite all the lights he knew were on, it seemed entirely dark and lonely — abandoned. More air magic illusions. Call was going to have to be careful to look out for other things that weren't really there.

He felt strange about leaving. It wasn't that he wanted to stay — he didn't like Master Joseph, he hated Alex, and Anastasia creeped him out — but he didn't like the idea of going back to prison either. And while Tamara might want to keep him safe, he didn't believe that was going to be easy.

The mage world wanted their revenge on Constantine and didn't care what happened to Callum.

He felt like no one cared about Call, only Constantine.

He heard the rustling of footsteps coming toward him and amended that grim thought. Tamara cared. Havoc cared.

Jasper sort of cared — or at least didn't think of Call as Constantine.

And Alastair cared. Maybe he and his father could leave the country. After all, Alastair had never wanted Call to fall into the hands of the mages — for this very reason. He was probably prepared. And the antique sales in Europe had to be pretty special.

"Call!" Tamara said, running up to him. "You made it."

Jasper looked at the Chaos-ridden and shivered. Havoc kept sniffing the air nervously. In the distance, there was a howl.

"He can help us some more," Call said, pointing to the Chaos-ridden. "Take us to the nearest, biggest road."

"Yesss," said the Chaos-ridden. "Thisss waaay."

Bracing himself for another long walk in the dark with his leg aching, Call pushed himself to his feet.

The five of them made their way by the moonlight as quickly as they could, Havoc scouting ahead and then doubling back. Call lagged behind. He wasn't used to walking anymore. His only exercise for several months had been pacing his cell and heading to the interrogation room. His leg burned.

Luckily, the Chaos-ridden matched his stride to Call's.

"They're going to notice we're gone," Jasper said, with a pleading look at Call. "They're going to come after us."

"I'm going as fast as I can," Call whispered back angrily. He hated that this had happened because of him and he was the one who was slowing them down.

"We won't be easy to find," Tamara said, with a glare at Jasper. "They don't know which way we went. And I bet they don't know we have a guide with us."

Call appreciated her sticking up for him, but he still felt bad. His spirits lifted a moment later, though, when the ground dipped down toward the inky-black asphalt of a road wide enough to have two lanes.

Havoc barked once in excitement.

"Shhhh!" Call said, although he was excited, too.

They scrambled down the hill.

"Um," Call told the Chaos-ridden. "I think you're going to have to wait here, okay? We'll come back and find you."

The Chaos-ridden immediately stopped moving, standing as still as some horrific statue. Call wondered if someone would drive by and try to stick him in the back of their trunk, the way Alastair often did with statues he found by the sides of roads.

"If there are cars," Jasper whispered as they hurried down the road, looking for a better-lighted place to try to catch a passing vehicle, "there must be a bridge, a way off this island . . ."

Call hadn't thought of that, but the logic lifted some of the pressure off his chest. Maybe they were closer to freedom than he'd thought. If there was a bridge and they could hitch a ride over it, then they were practically already out of Master Joseph's reach. He glanced up and down the road — seemingly deserted. They'd passed around a corner, so he could no longer see the Chaos-ridden.

Suddenly, lights swept toward them. Tamara gave a little gasp. It was a delivery van that read FLOWERS OF FAERIELAND in sickeningly sweet script along the side.

"A flower delivery van," said Jasper, sounding relieved. It did seem pretty unsinister, considering what else was on this island.

Tamara darted out into the middle of the road, waving her hands. She could have made a much bigger beacon with fire magic, Call thought, but that would have terrified an ordinary person.

The van pulled to a screeching halt. A middle-aged man with close-cropped hair and a backward baseball cap stuck his head out the window. "What's going on?"

"We're lost," Tamara said. She swept the newsboy cap off so her braids fell down, and batted her eyes innocently. With the pastel dress, she looked like someone who'd escaped an Easter egg hunt. "We rowed over to the island to look around, but our boat drifted away when we weren't looking and the sun went down. . . ." She sniffed. "Can you help us, mister?"

Call thought the *mister* was laying it on a little thick, but the guy seemed sold.

"Sure," the man said, looking bewildered. "I guess. Um, hop on up, kids."

As they approached, he threw out a ropy arm. There was a big black tattoo on his bicep that looked a little like an eye. It seemed weirdly familiar. "Whoa, whoa. What's that?" He pointed at Havoc.

"It's my dog," said Call. "His name's —"

"I don't care what his name is," said the guy. "He's huge."

"We really can't leave him." Tamara looked at the guy with huge eyes. "Please? He's really tame."

Which was how Call found himself, Jasper, and Havoc being loaded into the empty back of the truck, which had no seats, just windowless metal flooring and walls. Hugo (which was the guy's name) brought Tamara up to sit beside him in the cab. She threw Call and Jasper an apologetic look as Hugo pulled the metal door down, locking them in.

"Betrayed," said Jasper. "Once again, by a woman."

The truck started up. Call felt his muscles relax as soon as they were rolling. He might be sitting in pitch-black with Jasper, but he was getting away from Master Joseph and Alex.

"You know," he said, "that kind of attitude is not going to help you get Celia back."

A light sparked. It was a slight ember of fire magic, burning in Jasper's hand. It illuminated the inside of the truck and Jasper's thoughtful scowl.

"You know," he said, "it doesn't smell like flowers in here."

Now that he mentioned it, Call realized he was right. And there were no stray petals or stems on the floor near their feet. There was an odor in the van, but it was a chemical one — more like formaldehyde.

"I didn't like the look of that guy," said Jasper. "Or his tattoo."

Call suddenly remembered where he'd seen that eye

symbol before. Over the gates of the Panopticon. The prison that never slept. His heart thumped. Could the guy be a guard meant to take him back to prison?

In the front of the van, Call heard Tamara say, "No, not that way. No!"

Hugo said something in return. They hit a dirt road and started bumping around, so Call couldn't quite make out the words.

Then they lurched to a stop. After a moment, the back of the van opened.

Master Joseph stood at the foot, a stern expression on his face. Hugo had brought them back to the Enemy of Death's stronghold.

"Come along, Callum," he said. His voice was even and calm, but Call could see that his hands were in fists at his sides. He was furious, even if he didn't want Hugo to see it. "We must talk. I'd hoped to do this tomorrow and under better circumstances, but I can't have you wandering around the island."

Tamara climbed out of the passenger side, looking stricken. Call and Jasper clambered out of the back of the truck, followed by Havoc, who put his nose against the palm of Call's hand, clearly confused about everything that was happening.

Unfortunately, Call understood all too well. Master Joseph's prison wasn't the house — it was the whole island.

"It was an honor to kidnap you, sir," Hugo said to Callum with a wide grin. "You probably don't remember me, but I saw you in the Panopticon." He tapped the tattoo on his arm. "I was there, too, locked up, you know, ever since the war. Lots of us were. But once you came, we knew it was going to be all right. We never stopped believing in you, not even when they said you were dead. If anyone can rise, it's the Enemy of Death."

Jasper and Call looked at Tamara, who had her hands over her mouth. The strike on the Panopticon hadn't just been about freeing Call after all. Master Joseph had used Anastasia to help him get Constantine's old followers out, too.

"I don't want to be on this island," Call said. "Don't you think that if you're serving me, you should do what I want?"

"Thank you for bringing them back so swiftly," Master Joseph said, before Call's words could have any effect on Hugo.

Hugo grinned again, nodded to Call, and climbed back in his van. "Good luck getting your memories back," he said. "You'll remember soon enough why you want to be here."

With a heavy heart, Call watched the van pull away, taking their escape plan with it.

He was dejected enough to follow Master Joseph back into the house, with Tamara, Havoc, and Jasper behind him. Master Joseph took a key out of his pocket and unlocked a parlor they'd never been in before. It appeared to be unheated, easily as cold as it had been outside. There were double doors on the far side of the room and two couches in the center.

Master Joseph beckoned for them to sit, but remained standing.

"I could strip you of your magic and your life," Master Joseph said. "I could take your power for myself. Would you prefer that?"

"If that's what you were planning on doing, then what are you waiting for?" Call demanded.

Tamara and Jasper both half rose from the couch as if they thought a fight was coming. Havoc growled.

Master Joseph only laughed, though. "I have a proposal for you . . . how about that? Callum, once you complete the task I set for you, you can leave the island with your friends if that's what you still want."

"A task?" Call asked. "Is this some kind of trick thing where I have to tame an impossible elemental or separate dirt from sand on an entire beach?"

Master Joseph smiled. "Nothing like that." He flung open the doors at the far end of the room. After a moment, Call and the others joined him at the entryway.

Inside was a large, white-painted room. There was nothing in it but a metal table. On top of the table lay a body that was perfectly preserved, covered to the neck by a thin white sheet.

"The task," he said, "is to raise Aaron Stewart from the dead."

CHAPTER SIX

CALL HEARD TAMARA'S awful gasp. She staggered back, and Jasper caught her arm. Call couldn't have done it. He was completely frozen.

It was definitely Aaron on the table. He lay on his back. His blond hair had been brushed. His green eyes were open and blank.

Havoc put his head back and gave a single, awful howl of loneliness, abandonment, and horror. It was like he was making the sound Call couldn't make. It rang and rang in Call's ears as he stood there, his body beginning to shake.

"God, stop that noise —" It was Alex Strike, appearing in his black silk pajamas behind them. He looked rumpled and sleepy and annoyed, but the look turned quickly into a smirk.

"Oh. I see you decided to show them what's *really* going on here."

Tamara, Call, and Jasper watched with horror as he walked up to the table and yanked down the sheet. Aaron was wearing what they must have planned to bury him in — his Bronze Year uniform. Alex picked up one of his wrists. His wristband gleamed on it. Stones for heroism peppered the band, along with stones for his Iron, Copper, and Bronze Years. And the black stone of chaos, because he had been a Makar.

Much good it had done him, Call thought bitterly. Alex had stolen his magic and now he was only a shell — a shell that had once held life and animation and chaos and Aaron. "Don't touch him," Call growled.

Alex let go of Aaron's hand and it thumped lifelessly against the table. "Dead," he said, cheerfully. "*Muerto.*"

"I think we've got the message," said Jasper. "Thanks."

"What's going on?" said Tamara in a choked voice. "Why is Aaron here? The Magisterium is going to notice his body is missing!"

Master Joseph had been standing at the door, watching them with an eerie stillness. He came toward the center of the room now, his eyes flicking over Aaron's body as if it were something in a petri dish. "Oh, they already know. He was taken some time ago. They haven't said anything because it would hardly behoove them for the mage world to know they've messed this up, too. Losing the body of a dead Makar, after not noticing they had the Enemy of Death among them for three years? The Assembly would explode."

"To be fair to Call," said Jasper, "it really wouldn't have been very easy to guess he was the EOD. He's very wily."

Havoc had been pulling against Call's grip. Call let go. He felt too numb inside to care whether Havoc launched himself at Master Joseph and tried to bite his face.

But he didn't. Instead, Havoc went over to the table where Aaron's body lay, gave a heartbroken sniffle, and curled up under it.

"I don't understand," Tamara said, fighting tears. "What's the point of this? Nobody can raise the dead! Constantine couldn't and that's why we have the Chaos-ridden."

"Constantine *could* have," said Master Joseph. "He was but days away from that breakthrough when the Third Mage War broke out. Then, because of the Cold Massacre, he was forced to start again. But he — you — can do it now. The knowledge was in his soul, and his soul is here, in you, Call!"

Call looked at Aaron on the table. For the first time, what Master Joseph was saying didn't seem so crazy. Death was terrible — Alastair was still mourning Sarah and it had been more than a decade since she'd died. Call would have liked to have had a mom, even if she had some reservations about him. And all the people who hated him did so because Constantine Madden had taken someone from them. If he, Callum Hunt, could really bring people back from the dead — not halfway back, as with the creepy Chaos-ridden, but actually, really back — they would forgive him. They'd forgive him for anything.

And he could have Aaron for a best friend again. Aaron, alive and laughing. Aaron, reborn. Tamara wouldn't have to worry about making the wrong choice in saving him. Call could stop missing him. Everything could go back to the way it was.

"Here's the bargain I am prepared to make," Master Joseph continued. "Callum, you stay here and work to bring Aaron back from the dead. Alex will help you, since he is the architect of this unfortunate accident."

Call started to point out that Aaron's death was no accident and Alex was a murderer, but Master Joseph kept speaking.

"You will have access to Constantine's notes and my experience. Once you bring Aaron back, you can decide to take up your destiny to end death . . . or you can depart for good. If you choose to go, Callum, I will let you. I will accept that there isn't enough of Constantine Madden in you and I will release you from his destiny."

For a moment, Call wasn't sure he was hearing Master Joseph right. After all this effort, he would just let Call go?

"What about Tamara and Jasper?" Call asked. "And Aaron?"

"All of you," Master Joseph promised. "Tamara, Jasper, Aaron, Havoc. You can all leave. All I ask is this — you bring Aaron to the Assembly and let them see what we're capable of. If they still want war, so be it. But I have a feeling that seeing a loved one brought back to life will change their minds. Because if you can bring back your friend, you can bring back their friends, too. Their husbands and wives. Their parents. Their children. *Everyone* has lost someone. Everyone, deep in their hearts, wishes they could have a little more time to live."

Tamara cleared her throat. She had stopped looking over at Aaron on the table, although Call could tell she wanted to. "That seems fair," she said.

Call felt a wave of relief. He was glad it wasn't just him. If Tamara wanted to do it, then it must be okay to want it, too.

"But, Callum," Master Joseph went on, "if you find your heart stirred by what you've done, if you find the Assembly to be the cowards they are, afraid to plumb the depths of chaos magic and afraid to let anyone else do it either, then you must stay with us.

"Tamara and Jasper, I will train you while you are here. We need smart young mages like yourselves. You've heard a lot of things about the Enemy of Death's followers. You've probably been made to think that we're villains, but once you've been here for a time, you might come to see us differently, just as you've already been able to separate Call from the terrible stories about Constantine Madden."

"You're going to train us?" Jasper asked. "In what?"

Master Joseph smiled at him. "Perhaps you've forgotten that I taught at the Magisterium once. I turned out many fine apprentices, most of them completely uninterested in chaos magic. I taught the parents of some apprentices in the Magisterium today."

Call imagined those parents weren't exactly bragging now about having been Master Joseph's students. He wondered if their children knew.

"Do you accept this deal?" Master Joseph asked Call.

Call looked at Aaron's body and wanted to say yes. If there was any chance to bring back Aaron, he wanted to take it.

But this wasn't just a lot of points on his Evil Overlord list. This pretty much was the list. The whole thing. Saying yes to this made him an Evil Overlord. And not any Evil Overlord. It made him the Enemy of Death.

Still, Tamara hadn't objected and she wasn't objecting now. Even Jasper wasn't saying anything against it. They wanted Aaron back, too. Call knew they did. Constantine had wanted to bring his brother back but that had been different. Aaron was a good person. Aaron shouldn't be dead.

"Yes," Call said. "I'll do it. I'll bring him back."

Master Joseph's smile was electric. Alex, meanwhile, glowered menacingly.

"There is one complication I didn't mention," said Master Joseph.

"You can't change the deal," Tamara insisted.

"Oh no. Nothing like that." Everything friendly had gone out of Master Joseph's demeanor. He looked hard and cold and terrifying, like he had when Call had first met him. "It's only this — if you run again, I will destroy Aaron's body so that there's no chance he will ever come back. And if you run after that, I will kill one of you. I will stick to the terms of our deal, so long as you three stick to them as well."

Jasper drew a sharp breath. "You can't kill Call," he said. "You need him. He's your chaos mage."

"Alex also has the power of chaos now," Master Joseph replied in the same frightening voice. "And we have the Alkahest. Not only will I kill Call if I must, I have the means to do it. And to take his power."

He thought of Master Joseph's grim words at dinner: *Let's give Call an opportunity to find who he is — if he doesn't, I will strip the power from him myself.*

"I'm sure, however, that it won't come to that. Now, go to bed." The terrifying look was gone and Master Joseph was back to normal. At least, normal for him. "We will begin our studies in earnest in the morning."

With that, he ushered them away from Aaron's body, locking the door behind him.

With a last look back, Call headed toward the stairs. As he climbed them, he felt thoroughly exhausted. He'd started the day in prison and had ended it agreeing to do the one thing he'd thought he'd never do, try to raise the dead.

When he got to the top, he started toward the door to his room but wasn't sure if he could face it. He turned to Tamara, who was heading into the pink room.

"Can I sleep on your floor?" he asked. "Your room is the only non-creepy one."

"Me too?" asked Jasper, seizing on this idea.

Tamara gave a small smile. "Yeah. That would be good."

Jasper disappeared to get his sleeping things. Call did the same. After changing into pajamas, he dragged his mattress into Tamara's room, settling it against the legs of her footboard.

She was standing by the window in her own pajamas, which were white with lace ruffles. She looked up as Call came in and he saw how deeply shaken she looked.

He stopped dead. Tamara looked like she'd lost every ounce of her fighting spirit.

"W-what is it?" he asked.

"Aaron," she said. "It's awful enough that he died, but for Master Joseph to have stolen his body — the way he *looked*, all white and cold on that table —"

Call's feet moved without his conscious will. He couldn't just let her stand there looking so miserable. He went across the room toward her and reached out his hand, meaning to pat her shoulder. But the moment he got close to her, she threw her arms around his neck and buried her face in his chest.

Call stood stunned, barely breathing. His heart felt like an untethered balloon, bouncing around in his chest. He folded his arms around her carefully. She was small and warm. Sometimes he forgot how small she was, because her bravery loomed so large in his mind.

She smelled like soap and sunshine. He wanted to breathe her in but recognized that this would be seen as weird and possibly creepy behavior.

He thought of Anastasia's words and, despite the horror

they'd just come from, his pulse began to beat so hard he was afraid Tamara would notice it.

"Call," she said, her voice muffled. "I worried that once Aaron was gone you wouldn't be my friend anymore."

His heart thumped. "I was worried about the same thing."

"It's not true, though, right?" She looked up at him worriedly. "We're still friends. We're always going to be friends, no matter what."

He found himself gently patting her hair. Stroking it, even. He felt like he was someone else, not Callum Hunt. Someone who deserved to have Tamara Rajavi care about him. "Yeah," he said, surprised and slightly panicked by the words coming out of his mouth. "Ever since I first met you . . ."

The door flew open and Tamara and Call jumped apart as Jasper hastened in, wearing horse-covered pajamas and dragging a blanket. He curled up in it at the side of Tamara's bed as she walked back over to sit on the edge of her mattress. Call, looking nonchalant, sprawled on his own makeshift bed.

"I was just telling Call," Tamara said. "We have to be careful. Really careful."

"Is that news?" asked Jasper.

"Master Joseph is considering taking Call's power with the Alkahest," said Tamara. She turned to Call. "Think about it — then *Master Joseph* could *be* the Enemy of Death. He wouldn't need to try to make Call do what he wants; he could do it himself."

"But he values Constantine's soul," Jasper pointed out.

"I know," said Tamara. "He definitely thinks Call has a better chance of raising the dead," Tamara said. "Otherwise he would have taken Call's powers already. Which is why Call was smart to play along with Master Joseph about raising Aaron."

Play along? Call had been feeling as if he were floating; now he crashed back down to earth. Tamara had thought he was *playing along* with Master Joseph, that he hadn't meant anything he'd said about bringing back Aaron? But that had never crossed his mind. He'd thought they were in agreement. He'd thought that, for once, he wasn't doing the wrong thing.

They'd been so close just a moment before. Now it seemed all wrong, as though he'd tricked her somehow.

"We'll find a way out of here," Tamara told him now. "And we'll try to figure out how to get to the Alkahest. If we could steal it — or even better, destroy it — you'd be a lot safer. You just have to pretend to be trying to raise Aaron in the meantime."

"Yes!" Call said, more forcefully than he intended. "Pretend. Definitely. That's exactly what I was going to do."

But as he allowed himself to relax into sleep, with Havoc warm beside him, he already knew he was lying. He was still going to bring Aaron back from the dead.

Maybe it wasn't the right thing, but if everything could go back the way it was before, if Aaron could be alive and they could all be happy, he didn't care about right or wrong.

CHAPTER SEVEN

BREAKFAST THE NEXT morning was served by Chaos-ridden, as though Call and the others were attending the world's weirdest fancy boarding school. The Chaos-ridden plunked the dishes down hard, as though they were dropping rocks, causing food to occasionally bounce right off and into Havoc's mouth. Still, the table was piled high, with French toast dripping with butter, bacon and scrambled eggs, fresh-squeezed orange juice, and grits.

Tamara and Jasper were both on their best behavior, apparently in an attempt to convince Master Joseph they were Down With His Plan. Tamara had on a pale blue dress with only some of the lace ripped off, and there were horses on Jasper's shirt and pants.

Alex was there, too, though he didn't eat anything and just

drank black coffee. Call had a feeling Alex had an Evil Overlord list, too, but his scoring went the other way. He probably gave himself a point every time he dressed all in black or menaced small children. Maybe a gold star if he did both at once.

After breakfast, Master Joseph took Jasper and Tamara off for lessons in the library, while Alex — jittery from coffee — and Call returned to the room where they'd left Aaron's body.

They didn't talk on the way. Call had resigned himself to spending time with Alex, though there wasn't anyone in the world he hated more. Alex had lied to him for years, had killed his best friend, had taken Aaron away from him. Call wouldn't be sorry to see him dead. He knew that was Evil Overlordian of him, but he accepted it — even as he reminded himself that Alex was also his path *back* to Aaron. He knew more about Constantine's methods than Call did.

Call couldn't decide if he was relieved or not when it turned out that Aaron's body had been taken away. Instead, there was a different metal table in the room. On it lay something small and stiff and dead.

Call recoiled. "Yerk," he said. "What's that?"

"Common garden stoat," said Alex, pacing behind the table. "We get to raise it. Something to practice on." He lifted an eyebrow at Call's expression. "This is necromancy, Callum. It can get messy and dangerous. And once Aaron's body is damaged, it can't be repaired."

"How did Master Joseph steal Aaron's body, anyway?" Call asked as Alex went over to a shelf and took down two pairs of heavy canvas gloves. He tossed one pair to Call and took the other.

"Anastasia was in the Magisterium after the funeral," said Alex. "She arranged with Master Joseph to release an air elemental who carried the body here." He grinned as he yanked the black gloves on. "I bet you could have heard those Masters screaming through the whole cave system."

"So you don't miss it, I guess," Call said, putting on his own gloves. "The Magisterium. Kimiya."

"Kimiya?" Alex burst out laughing. "You think I'm pining away over Kimiya? You think I feel badly about lying?"

"I guess it would have been awkward to tell her you were a murderer in thrall to Master Joseph," said Call.

Alex raised an eyebrow. "I didn't notice you running around blurting your little secret to everyone, *Constantine*."

"Well," said Call, "they all know now."

Alex gave him an odd look. "Yeah, they do. And Kimiya knows about me." He bent over the stoat. "So."

"So," echoed Call. "Time to share your wisdom. How do you raise the dead?"

"Anastasia said you brought back Jen Matsui," said Alex.

"Yeah, but she was . . . Chaos-ridden." Call shuddered. "She was all wrong."

"She was able to answer questions. Chaos-ridden can't do that. It's a start."

Call frowned at Alex. Of course Chaos-ridden could answer questions. They could talk! Did that mean that Alex couldn't hear them?

Now that Call thought about it, it was weird that Jen had come back being able to be heard by everyone. Did that mean Call had done something different with her, something Alex wasn't doing with his own Chaos-ridden?

Call held up his gloved hands. "I thought you were the expert here. I thought you'd been 'practicing with Constantine's methods' or whatever."

"I know a lot," Alex said angrily. "For starters, we're chaos mages. Chaos is unstable energy. Our instinct is to grab that chaos and shove it into an empty body without a soul. That's how you get Chaos-ridden."

"Uh-huh." Call nodded, following so far, although the part about instinct was creepy.

"But every element has access to its opposite. And the opposite of chaos is the soul. The human stuff that makes people who they are. Stoats, too." Alex looked as if he was amusing himself. "We've got to reach out there and find this weasel's little weasel soul and shove it back into its body, just like Constantine shoved his soul into you."

"Right," Call said, remembering how it had felt to look for Jennifer Matsui's soul. He and Aaron had caught traces of it to make her talk, but then it had started to fade away, back into nothing. He had grabbed for it and it had come apart in pieces. How he'd channeled magic into those shining threads to hold on to it.

She had woken up Chaos-ridden.

"Right," Alex said, like Call wasn't listening.

"That's it?" Call demanded. He was realizing, with dawning horror, that Alex didn't know more than he did about bringing back the dead.

And what did that mean, when Alex was supposed to have been studying Constantine's methods and Call had stumbled into the same — or possibly even a better — technique? Was Master Joseph right about Call — did having Constantine's soul make him *automatically* better at raising the dead?

Alex stared at Call with a superior expression on his face. "You might not think it's much, but it's not as easy as it sounds."

Call sighed. "I already tried it."

"What?" Alex frowned. "You have not —"

Call didn't care about Alex or his attitude. "That's how I brought back Jennifer. I didn't mean for her to come back Chaos-ridden. There just wasn't enough of her soul left."

For a moment, Call thought Alex was going to hit him. "I know things, *secret things*," he said, stabbing a finger toward Call.

It was clear, though, that he didn't. "If what you're saying actually worked, then we wouldn't have to do any experiments. Master Joseph said Constantine was on the verge of a breakthrough, not that he'd had one." Call sighed. "I want to see Constantine's notebooks myself."

"Why?" Nothing about this situation was going Alex's way, but he was clearly unwilling to give an inch.

Call was tired of arguing. "If you don't let me see them, Master Joseph will."

"Let's just try to bring back this stoat," Alex said. "Come on — concentrate."

"I don't know —" Call said.

"Then I'm going to do it myself." Alex closed his eyes tightly, as though he were trying to burst a vein in his forehead.

Call could feel the chaos magic in the air, could almost smell it, like a hot wind.

On the table, the stoat began to stir. It shuddered all over. Its back paws pinwheeled. Its whiskers quivered. And then it opened swirling eyes.

Chaos-ridden.

Alex opened his own eyes expectantly, but when he saw what was on the table, he slammed his fist against the wall.

"You should have helped me," he said. "What we need is more power!"

The stoat jumped off the table and was making for the door when Havoc roused himself from sleep and began to chase after it. Call heard something smash, then a high-pitched cry.

"And a different stoat," Call told Alex, vowing to never let him anywhere near Aaron's body.

↑ ≈ △ ○ ◎

They decided to break for lunch, though Call wasn't exactly hungry. *Several hours with a dead stoat will do that to you*, he thought.

As Alex headed for the dining room, Call pulled off toward the kitchen to get something quick . . . and to not have to see Alex while he ate. There, he found a young man putting tea things on a tray.

"Hello," the young man said.

Call, not wanting to be rude, said, "Hi."

Seeing Call's confusion, the young man laughed without guile and said, "My name is Jeffrey and I help out around here. I didn't pass the tests to get into the Magisterium, but Master Joseph offered to teach me anyway, instead of having my magic bound."

"Oh," Call said. He had to admit, that was a pretty good way of getting recruits, although Call wasn't sure how much magic they could learn. But what if the answer was a lot? Call thought of Hugo driving the van, of all the prisoners in the Panopticon, and wondered how many people were on the island.

"You're Callum, right?" Jeffrey asked.

"Yeah," he said.

"Come with me. Assemblywoman Tarquin wanted me to bring you to her when you came out of your lessons."

Call wasn't sure exactly what Jeffrey thought he'd been doing, but he followed to a small Victorian parlor where Jeffrey set his tray of tea and sandwiches down on a table between two big velvet armchairs.

There was a large bay window that looked out at the green lawn where a Chaos-ridden pushed a lawn mower in a strange pattern on the grass. Presiding over the room was Anastasia, wearing another of her white power suits. She gestured for Call to sit down in the armchair opposite her.

Jeffrey left and Call took his place awkwardly. The silver stand of iced cakes and crustless sliced sandwiches was between them. He took an egg salad one and held it gingerly.

"You must be very angry with me," Anastasia said.

"You think?" Call took a bite of the sandwich. On the whole he preferred lichen. "You mean, because you lied to Tamara and betrayed us and let Master Joseph kidnap us? Why would I be mad about that?"

Her lips tightened. "Call," she said. "You were in the Panopticon. I had to do what I could to get you out. Do you think there was going to be any freedom for you? No. You would have been pursued by the mages from the moment they realized you were missing."

"I don't see the difference between them catching me and Master Joseph catching me," Call argued. "This is just prison with sandwiches."

"In my life," said Anastasia, "I have learned that allegiances don't matter. You can be destroyed by those who call themselves good as easily as by those who are more obviously selfish. All that matters to me, Call, is that you remain alive and safe." She leaned forward. "Do as Master Joseph says. He will help you raise Aaron from the dead. Then, once you have him back, you can go before the Magisterium and show what you've done. Do you truly think that they will reject such a gift? Everyone hates death, Call."

"But not everyone has to be its enemy."

She shook her head. "You don't understand. I'm saying they'll accept you. They'll embrace you as their Makar, just as they'll embrace your magic and use it to bring back their loved ones. You'll no longer be in any danger."

"I don't know if that'll work," he muttered, but she didn't seem like she heard him.

"I've filled your room with your things — with Constantine's things," she said. "I know you're still fighting who you really are. It's ironic, because Con was always stubborn." Her eyes were soft as she looked at him. "You've buried what you are for so long. Just let the pictures and clothes surround you — let your soul remember." She sighed. "I wish I could stay. I'd tell you stories about yourself every day, about what Constantine did when he was a little boy."

This sounded like the worst thing Call could think of. "You're leaving?" he said warily.

"I must return to the Magisterium and give them a good story about how you were taken and I escaped with my life. Hopefully, I can be convincing enough so that I can keep an eye on their plans a little longer."

"What if I can't do what Master Joseph wants?" Call asked her, thinking of Aaron's cold body on the table. Yes, he wanted Aaron back, but he wasn't going to let Alex raise Aaron as one of the Chaos-ridden. He'd do whatever he had to do in order to make sure that never happened. "Constantine couldn't bring back the dead — maybe I can't either. If I fail, Master Joseph is going to use the Alkahest to take my power."

Anastasia gave him a searching look. "Master Joseph needs you. He will use the Alkahest to take your power only if he is forced into a corner. Don't force him into a corner, Call. He needs us — and we need him."

"You don't mind him threatening me?" Call said. "You don't think we should be worried?"

"If I thought there was a safer place to go, I would go there," said Anastasia. "But your soul, your restless soul, Con, was never meant to have peace. It was meant to have power." She moved closer to him. "You are powerful. You can't just give up that power. The world won't let you. It won't allow you to simply hide and be safe. It may come to this — ruling the world or being crushed under its boot heel."

That seemed grim and dramatic, but Call just nodded, trying to look thoughtful instead of freaked out. Anastasia touched his cheek once, longingly, and then rose. "Good-bye, my dear."

As weird as she acted around him, and as much as he didn't want her talking about how much he was like Constantine all the time, he was a little sorry to see her go. Anastasia wanted him to *be* Constantine, her lost son, and that wasn't possible, but at least he felt like she was kind of on his side.

Master Joseph wasn't, no matter how he pretended to be.

Call ate the rest of his egg salad sandwich alone, watching the Chaos-ridden push the mower right into the river.

After that, he looked around the house for Tamara and Jasper, hoping he could persuade Master Joseph that they could all learn together. When he didn't find them, he went back to the stoat room. Alex was there, with two new, partially defrosted stoats.

Call felt a little queasy.

"Here," Alex said, slamming a black notebook stuffed with extra sheets of loose-leaf paper onto the table. "This was Constantine's final notebook. And if you want to see the others, you don't have far to look. They're in your room, on your bookshelves, just like Master Joseph and Anastasia insisted."

"Thanks," Call said grudgingly, picking up the book.

"Now it's your turn," Alex said, pointing to the small creatures on the table.

Call looked at the stoats. He wasn't sure he could do it. But he did want Aaron back. And if there was any chance . . .

He reached out with chaos magic, toward one of the creatures. He could sense the cold that still gripped it, could feel the silvery remains of where its soul had been. Something was still there.

He tried to catch hold of it, tried to warm it and grow it to life. But there was too little left. In desperation, he tried to inflate what was there. *We need more power*, Alex had said.

Call inhaled, gathering up the chaos inside himself, reaching into the darkness and the violence and the swirling movement that only a Makar could see. He grabbed at the chaos as if with both hands, shoving it desperately into the inflated soul of the stoat as if he were trying to light a fire in the middle of an ice field.

He felt the spark catch, and grow —

Alex yelled. Call ducked down as a loud bang echoed through the room. When he stood up again, black spots danced in front of his eyes. He felt weak and exhausted, drained of energy and magic.

Alex looked at him furiously. He was splattered with bits of an unspeakable something that Call didn't want to dwell on.

"You exploded the stoat," Alex said.

"I did?" Call was amazed, but the unfortunate evidence was everywhere. He'd missed the worst of it by ducking under the table, but Alex and his designer jeans hadn't been so lucky.

Alex took off his gloves and threw them down on the table. "I am so done with today."

He stalked out, and after a minute, Call followed. Nobody wanted to be alone in a room with two dead stoats, one of them in pieces.

He hoped Jeffrey wouldn't get stuck cleaning up.

"How did it go?" Master Joseph asked that night at dinner.

They were all gathered in the dining room again, though Anastasia's chair was empty. The table groaned with food: potato salad, coleslaw, barbecue ribs gleaming with spicy sauce, beans simmered in molasses, emerald collard greens. Jasper had already eaten an entire rack of ribs.

"Call exploded a stoat," Alex reported. He looked freshly scrubbed, as if he'd showered and then showered again.

"One cannot expect to get everything right in the beginning," said Master Joseph, gnawing a rib. "But I expect you to make steady progress."

"I'm sure someone else could do just as well as Call at this," said Alex. He was staring piercingly at Master Joseph, as if to communicate his hope that Master Joseph would immediately suck out Call's powers with the Alkahest and move on from there.

"I'm sure they couldn't," said Master Joseph, though his jaw tightened. Call watched him in fascination.

Did Master Joseph ever want to use the Alkahest and have Chaos magic for himself? First, he'd been in Constantine's shadow, and now he was in Call's. Did it ever bother him? It was hard to tell; his voice was calm when he said, "We've never had two Makars before working on this project. Even Constantine was alone."

I'm definitely alone, Call thought. Alex was worse than no help at all. But Alex just grinned at him across the table in a not-pleasant way.

"We'll get right on it tomorrow," Alex said.

After dinner, Tamara and Jasper spilled into Call's bedroom to swap information about their days. Master Joseph had been teaching them how to form solid and unbreakable surfaces out of air and water.

But as Call had begun to realize after meeting Jeffrey, they weren't the only ones being taught. There were other mages, with other groups. Hugo taught ten younger students, and Tamara and Jasper had spotted at least four other apprentice groups — apprentice groups larger than the ones allowed at the Magisterium. Jeffrey was probably teaching, too.

"He wouldn't let us make sharp things, though," Jasper said. "Though I guess that makes sense. He doesn't want us armed. We figured out there's some kind of air elemental forming the protections around the Alkahest — like a guardian." He forced a smile. "But that's okay. We'll figure out a way around it."

"What about you, Call?" Tamara looked at him anxiously. "Was it really bad?"

Call paused near the bookshelf. On it were rows and rows of photos of Constantine and his friends. It was hard not to notice that in every one of them, Constantine was laughing at the center of a group. People were always looking at him. "It was fine," he lied. "I'm just pretending to try anyway."

"I'm going to try to get close to Master Joseph," Jasper said. "Act like I am getting into his whole evil thing so that I can see if he'll tell me stuff. After all, their whole plan can't be to raise Aaron from the dead. That's not enough to take over the world."

"You think he has an army?" Call asked. "I mean, beyond the prisoners and the students. An army of Chaos-ridden?"

"*Everyone* thinks he's got an army," Jasper replied. "But we all thought the Enemy of Death was still alive, creating more and more Chaos-ridden. If the only person who can make more of them is Alex, then maybe his army isn't that big."

Call looked over and saw Tamara was looking at a picture on his dresser — one of his parents and Constantine.

"It's funny to look at them," Tamara said. "You would never know one of these apprentices was going to tear the mage world apart."

Call glanced in the mirror. He hadn't remembered to brush his hair that morning and there was a barbecue stain on his shirt. He didn't look like much of a threat either, but had the uncomfortable feeling that the next few weeks were going to define his destiny.

Despite having the meeting in Call's room, they all moved to Tamara's to sleep. But as the others dropped off into slumber, Call found himself staring at the ceiling, his wolf cuddled up to his side. *Your soul*, Anastasia had said. *Your restless soul was never meant to have peace.*

You don't know me, Call thought. *You don't know my soul.* He rolled over and closed his eyes tightly, but it was still a long, long time before he dropped off to sleep.

CHAPTER EIGHT

ALEX MIGHT HAVE hoped for big things, but the second day went even worse than the first. Call spent half of it looking through Constantine's notes, which had been made in neat columns that caused Call to despair of his own handwriting. If you were going to get someone's soul, Call thought, it would be nice if you also got their superior penmanship. Constantine had written down lots of numbers, indicating experiments and then measurements, which appeared to be chaos-related. He determined the minimum energy that was required to bring back one of the Chaos-ridden and then lists of improvements you could get with more chaos and more delicate handling of the soul.

Speaking was one of them, which annoyed Alex.

But the spirit — the essence of what was missing in a person — seemed to be something Constantine hadn't been able to define or re-create. Despite Master Joseph's insistence that they'd been close to a breakthrough, Call didn't see anything in the list of experiments that actually indicated this.

What Constantine had actually done was to push his own existing soul into someone else's body. That was impressive magic and it had saved Constantine's life, but it wasn't bringing back the dead.

That night, at dinner, both Jasper and Tamara appeared worked up in a way that puzzled Call. They seemed to be buzzing with a weird energy, and Tamara kept shooting Significant Looks over to Call, gesturing over the homemade pasta. He had no idea what she was trying to communicate.

He thought of Anastasia's claim that Tamara had a crush on him. When Celia had liked him, she had done lots of confusing and inexplicable things. Maybe Anastasia was right . . . but that still didn't explain what Tamara wanted him to *do*.

"We made progress today," Alex lied. He gazed at Master Joseph as if hoping for approval.

Master Joseph just looked at Call. "Don't force it," he said. "Relax. The ability is there."

Call stared at Tamara. She was miming something to do with a cat. *Cat?* he mouthed at her, and she nodded, then mimed brushing her hair. Call was flummoxed. There was a cat in the house and she wanted him to brush it? Call liked cats, but Havoc regarded them as more of a delicacy. No cat would sit still to be brushed around a giant, Chaos-ridden wolf. What was Tamara thinking?

Unless it was a Chaos-ridden cat . . . Had Tamara found a Chaos-ridden cat?

"I really think we could make some advances," Alex went on. "Change the way magic is done."

He glanced at Tamara, as if he was hoping *she'd* be impressed. Which made Call furious. He stopped paying attention to Tamara's gesturing and glared at Alex, wishing he could punch him.

Call was jealous. Jealous of Alex because he was the kind of boy that people liked. Call knew Tamara hated Alex for killing Aaron and even if that had never happened, she *still* wouldn't like Alex, because he had made her sister cry. He knew all that, but it didn't help.

Whether or not Tamara actually had a crush on Call, it didn't matter. Call liked her.

He liked her and he was going to have to tell her.

"So," said Jasper, noting the strained silence. He gestured toward the sideboard. "Anyone for that chocolate cake?"

After dinner, Jasper, still working on his plan to impress Master Joseph, asked if the older mage could show him how to create the force fields of air that barred the windows. Alex, who was an air mage, immediately offered to co-teach.

"You're not going to be able to use this information to escape, you know," Alex said with obvious pleasure. "It's very advanced stuff. Besides, even if you got out of the house, you'd never make it off the island."

"Oh no," Jasper said. "I wasn't thinking of trying to escape."

Master Joseph gave him an indulgent smile. "Of course not. Come along." He led the way to one of the practice rooms.

The moment they disappeared, Tamara grabbed Call's hand. "Come on," she hissed, and dragged him out of the dining room, into the parlor. She shut the door and leaned against it.

"I have to tell you something," she said, looking around as if someone might be lurking in the shadows, spying. She was wearing another pastel dress, this one pale apricot, with a lace skirt.

This was it. She was about to tell Call she liked him.

No, he should tell her first. Because once she got talking he was going to go all tongue-tied and make a fool of himself. He was going to get caught up in saying the right thing and might not be able to say anything at all.

"I like you!" he blurted out. "I think you're pretty and I like you and I always liked you, even back when you really didn't like me. You're brave and smart and great and I think I am going to stop talking now."

"There are tunnels under the house," Tamara said at nearly the same time.

The floor seemed to tilt under his feet. She hadn't been about to confess her feelings. In fact, she was looking at him as though he was some new species of bug that she'd never encountered before.

His face heated. "Tunnels?" he echoed numbly.

"Jasper and I eavesdropped and heard Hugo and Master Joseph talking about them. Apparently deliveries come in through there, and they store extra supplies there, too. They called them the catacombs." She spoke a bit stiltedly, as though stunned by his news.

"Oh," said Call, realizing belatedly what Tamara's gesturing had been about. "You were trying to mime *catacomb*."

"I'm sorry," she said. "But if we're going to explore them, we have to go there now, if we're going to go. While Jasper is keeping Master Joseph distracted. We can talk later."

"I'm ready to go," said Call, trying to act normal. "But we don't need to talk about what I said. Like, ever."

Anastasia had been wrong — of course she'd been wrong. Tamara didn't like him. She'd never had a crush on him.

He'd only believed it because he'd wanted it to be true.

Tamara gave Call a small smile and pushed past him to the center of the room. A thick Persian rug was on the floor. She started to roll it up, revealing the square of a trapdoor underneath. She glanced up. "Come and help me."

Call went over and knelt down by her, his leg twinging. For several minutes they wrestled with the door, trying to find a handle or a pressure point or anything that would open it.

Finally, Call bit his lip. "Let me try something," he said.

He placed his hand on top of the door and thought hard

about the chaos magic he'd been doing, the reaching through the void to try to find something. The wild, churning emptiness of the chaos element. He drew that darkness up, as if he were lifting smoke, and let it flow down out of his hand.

Blackness like ink spilled across the trapdoor. It gave a twitch under Call's hand and vanished, ripped away into the void, revealing a ladder leading downward.

Tamara exhaled. "Was that hard?" she whispered.

"No," Call said. It was true. Using chaos magic had once been difficult, but now it was becoming more and more like using any other element. He didn't know if that should scare him or not.

The only problem was, he'd just eaten away a section of the floor, so if someone walked across the rug, they'd fall into a hole. But right now, brokenhearted, he wasn't sure he could bring himself to care.

At least they were friends, he told himself. At least they would always be friends.

They climbed down into a long, dark tunnel with stone walls. Master Rufus had always taught him that chaos was not in itself evil. It was an element like any other. But there were plenty of places where Makars were killed at birth because chaos had so much power to destroy. It was why Anastasia had moved Constantine to America after he was born, to save his life.

And look how that turned out.

Tamara had lit a small flame in the palm of her hand. They were navigating by it, the orange light picking out the twists and turns of the corridors, the many rooms that led off them. Most were empty. Some contained stacked crates or jars that were clearly meant to hold elementals. One held a pile of steel chains that Call recognized; Master Joseph had once used them to imprison Aaron.

Tamara paused in front of one door. "In here," she said in a low voice.

They stepped inside, and Call immediately saw what she'd noticed. A bow and arrow hung on one wall, and a sharp lance was propped against another. The whole room was a jumble of weird items — books, photo albums, boys' clothes, furniture, sports equipment.

A cold feeling had set up house in Call's stomach. Tamara had picked up a dagger with some initials etched on it — *JM*.

"Jericho Madden," he said. "This must be Jericho's stuff."

"What's it doing down here?" she asked.

Call frowned. "Probably Constantine had it stored for when he brought his brother back."

It must have been here for maybe twenty years. And now that Jericho's body was destroyed, it would be down here for a lot longer.

Call couldn't help wondering where Aaron's stuff was, but he couldn't talk about that. It would definitely tip her off that he was considering bringing Aaron back.

Aaron, who would definitely not laugh if Call told him the stupid thing he had done.

Okay, Aaron hadn't been perfect. He might have laughed.

Pushing all those thoughts away, Call lifted stacks of things and looked around. He found a few schoolbooks and novels and then a small, unmarked leather notepad. Call opened it. The handwriting looked like it belonged to a teenage boy. Drawings of lizards and other kids decorated the edges of the pages. Unlike Constantine's notes, these weren't just graphs and experiments.

I am doing a special project with Master Joseph and Con. Master Rufus gave me this book and told me to take notes on what happens, so that's what I am going to do. So far, being the brother of the Makar means I get shuffled off wherever he goes. I am barely considered a mage in my own right anymore. Everyone only considers me his counterweight. No one wants to know how weird it is to feel his soul pulling at my own.

Call held the book up with a shudder to show Tamara. "Jericho kept a diary," he told her.

Tamara's eyebrows rose. She was looking at a Polaroid that she turned toward Call. It was of Anastasia with two little boys dressed in white. In the photograph, Anastasia had on a flowered dress and was sitting in the grass, unsmiling. Tamara turned it over. Someone had written the year on the back.

With a sigh, since Call knew how all of this turned out, he tucked the diary into a pocket of his flannel, to be read later.

"Maybe there's something here they overlooked," Tamara said. "Something they wouldn't let us have on our own, but they kept for him?"

"Like a tornado phone?" Call asked, thinking of the one on

Master Rufus's desk he'd used to contact his father when he'd first come to the Magisterium.

"Too good to hope for," Tamara said.

They searched and searched, but they didn't find anything else that seemed useful. The only thing remotely interesting was a bunch of old books about Makars from all over the world and their dubious achievements. A few of them had been called things like the Scythe of Souls, the Hooded Kestrel, Devourer of Men, the Maw, Shaper of Flesh, the Scourge of Luxembourg, and the Face Harvester — definitely inspirations for Constantine's "Enemy of Death." Several claimed to have discovered the secret of immortality, among other scary things, but obviously, the books didn't actually tell you what the secrets were. Finally, Tamara sat down on a nearby chair.

"We should probably go back before anyone notices we're missing," she said.

Call nodded, suddenly conscious that they were alone, and that he'd just poured out his heart to her. No Jasper around to make snide comments, or Master Joseph or Alex to stare creepily. Just him and Tamara.

"Look, Tamara," he said. "Everything I said before, it was dumb. You probably liked Aaron. You probably didn't even mean to save me instead of him. You probably have a lot of regrets."

Tamara reached out and took one of Call's hands. He wasn't conscious of how cold he'd grown until he felt the warmth of her skin. "I wake up in the night sorry I didn't save Aaron. But, Call — I'm not sorry I saved you."

He couldn't quite draw a breath. "You're not sorry?"

She leaned toward him. Their faces were very close together. He could see her small Fatima necklace glittering around her throat. "I thought you knew how I felt."

"How you felt?" Call wondered if he was doomed to repeat everything she said. She was clutching both of his hands now, nervously. Her eyes were huge and dark and fixed on him.

"*Call*," Tamara said, and he kissed her. He wasn't sure later what prompted him or suggested to him it would be a good idea. He had no idea what instinct told him he wouldn't get slapped or, worse, informed that he was a really good friend but Tamara just didn't feel that way about him.

But neither of those things happened. Tamara made a little noise and moved to adjust into a better position and what had been Call pressing his mouth nervously against Tamara's became something else. Something that made it feel like his heart was exploding inside his chest. She put her hands lightly against either side of his face and the kiss went on for so long that Call's ears were roaring.

Finally, they pulled apart. Tamara was blushing bright red but looked pleased. And Call felt happy. For the first time since Aaron had died, he felt happy.

He'd almost forgotten what it was like.

I just had my first kiss in a stronghold of the Enemy of Death, in a room full of his dead brother's stuff, Call thought. *Story of my life.*

He didn't mind, though. For the moment, he didn't mind anything.

"Let's go," Tamara said. Her cheeks had faded to pink. "Before anyone comes into the parlor and notices we opened the trapdoor."

Call disagreed. He thought they should stay and kiss some more. It was an underrated invention, or at least one he hadn't rated highly enough himself until this minute.

Tamara put her hand in his, and in a sort of daze, Call followed her out the door and back through the catacombs, holding hands tightly. Holding hands was also surprisingly awesome. Every time they turned a corner she squeezed his fingers and sent small bolts of lightning zipping up his arm.

They had to separate when they got to the ladder that went up to the parlor. Tamara climbed up first, and Call after, and they were distracted for a while cleaning up the room and making it look like they'd never been there. They found some boards to brace over the hole that seemed like they might hold someone's weight.

They crept out of the room and up the stairs. Call was about to see if Tamara was maybe up for more hand-holding when Jasper loomed up at them out of the shadows. "Where have you *been*?" he demanded.

Call glared. Jasper was always going on and on about romance — you'd think he'd notice when he wasn't wanted. But then Jasper had always been oblivious to his many severe personality defects.

"We explored the catacombs just like we planned," Tamara said, nodding toward where they'd come from. At that moment, Call remembered that Jasper and Tamara spent all day together, planning things.

Jealousy flared up again, even though he'd just been kissing her. After all, Jasper was Tamara's old friend and he had somehow convinced the last girl who liked Call to like him better.

The thought was like a splash of cold water. Abruptly he realized several things: (1) Kissing created a haze of stupidity that lasted for at least ten minutes; (2) now that it had worn off, he had no idea what kissing Tamara meant; and (3) he had no idea what he was supposed to do now.

All of a sudden, Call had an overwhelming urge to grab Jasper by the collar and force him to divulge all his romantical secrets. Previously, Call had scoffed at them, but now he was ready to listen unskeptically.

"Well, I stalled as much as I could but you better get up to our rooms before Master Joseph notices you're missing," Jasper said. Then his annoyance faded. "Did you find anything?"

Tamara nodded. They started up toward the pink room, Call trailing behind. Sleeping in the same room made him feel weird. He recalled sleeping next to her on the cot in Alastair's car barn. That had been a little strange, but nothing like it was going to be just to share a room now.

Tamara was beautiful, brave, awesome. He thought she was destined to go out with someone heroic like Aaron, or throwing herself away on a jerky aristocrat like Jasper. The idea that she liked him after all, when he had been sure she did, then was sure she didn't, still had his head reeling.

He gave Jasper the side-eye thinking about jerky aristocrats, as he settled himself on his mattress on the floor. Tamara went into the bathroom and came out in purple pajamas with ruffles at the shoulders.

Just looking at her made his chest ache in a new, panicky way. If there was one thing he knew about himself, it was that he could take any good thing and make a mess out of it.

"What did you find?" Jasper asked.

"Jericho's diary," Call said. "I haven't read it yet, but maybe there's something in there." He paused, realizing that what he was hoping for in the diary wasn't anything the others were interested in. "I mean, about getting to the Alkahest or getting off this island or the missing army."

"We should go back and see if there's something we missed," Tamara said.

Was that an invitation to more kissing? Call couldn't be sure. He looked her way, but she was staring up at the ceiling.

Jasper nodded. "I've been sticking tight to Master Joseph,

but so far the only thing I've discovered is his chili recipe. The lesson on magical force fields wasn't very informative."

Call hadn't bothered changing his clothes for bed. He stretched out on his mattress, his head full of the kiss and all the confusion that came with it.

"Good night, Call," Tamara said with a smile that seemed to have a lot of secrets in it.

Jasper gave him a weird look. Call decided that tomorrow, he would demand that Jasper explain everything he knew about girls. Call only hoped it wasn't too late.

For once, his dreams weren't full of chaos.

CHAPTER NINE

WHEN TAMARA, JASPER, and Call woke up in the morning, the boys retreated to their own rooms to shower and change for breakfast. Call waved at Tamara as he left, but she didn't seem to notice.

After a quick shower, Call yanked the day's selection of Constantine's clothes out of the closet with distaste — another day, another flannel shirt. He wished he had his own stuff to wear.

As he pulled his jean jacket back on, Jericho's diary fell out of the inner pocket. Call picked it up, turning it over slowly in his hands. Constantine's brother had owned this book. Had written in it. Call had never thought of Jericho as a person, had never really thought of him at all. Even when he had stood over Jericho's preserved body in the tomb of the Enemy, he had thought only about what Constantine must have felt when his brother had died.

But now he was counting on Jericho's diary to give him an insight that Constantine's notes had failed to provide.

A knock came on the door. There was just time for Call to slip the book back into his pocket before Jasper stuck his head in.

"Hugo came by," he said, sauntering into Call's room without permission. "He said Tamara and I have a free afternoon once our morning lessons are over. He's going to go somewhere with Master Joseph, and I'm going to follow them." He looked narrowly at Call. "Are you listening?"

"I want to know everything you know about girls," said Call.

"I knew you would bow to my superior knowledge of romance eventually." Jasper appeared smug.

"How do you let a girl know you like her?" said Call. "And if you kiss one, does that mean you're in a relationship?"

Jasper leaned back against the wall, his hand under his chin. "That depends, my man," he said, squinting as if he were wearing a monocle. "How well do you know the lady?"

"Very well," said Call, fighting the urge to tell Jasper he looked like Mr. Peanut.

Jasper frowned. "It's weird that you're asking me this now," he said, "given that we're stuck out here in the middle of nowhere with no girls around except . . . Tamara." A look of shock dawned on his face. "You and *Tamara*?"

Call bristled. "Does that seem so unlikely?"

"Yes," Jasper said. "Tamara's your friend. She isn't — she doesn't feel that way about you."

"Because I'm the Enemy of Death?" Call snapped. "Because I'm rotten inside and don't deserve her? Thanks, Jasper. Thanks a lot."

Jasper looked at him without speaking for a long moment. "Do you know why Celia and I broke up?" he asked, finally.

"She got tired of your face?"

"I said I was going to visit you in prison, and she said I couldn't. She said if you were the Enemy of Death, you were a murderer. She said I had to choose between you and her."

Call blinked. Part of him felt hurt, even now, by Celia's words, a distant, deep-down ache. The rest of him was astonished by Jasper. "*You* stood up for me?"

Jasper seemed to regret saying anything. "I don't like being told what to think."

Call didn't want to feel grateful to Jasper, but he did. Overwhelmingly grateful. "Thanks," he said.

Jasper waved his words away. "Yes, yes, but the important point I'm making is that when I say that Tamara doesn't like you that way, I'm not saying it because I think you're a bad person. I just think Tamara — well, Call, I just think she liked *someone else*, if you get my meaning."

Aaron. He meant Aaron.

Call wanted to protest that *Anastasia* thought Tamara liked him, but he could just imagine what Jasper would say to that — that Anastasia had no idea what she was talking about at the best of times and certainly didn't seem like an expert on love. And Tamara hadn't looked at Call that morning, hadn't said much to him since the kissing. And she hadn't said how she felt about him, only that she thought he knew.

Jasper looked thoughtful. "And if she sucked face with you, it was probably because she didn't want to die alone and respected Celia too much to throw herself at me."

It wasn't like that at all, Call wanted to say. "But I could still ask her to be my girlfriend, right?" After all, even if it was a mistake, maybe it was one she would want to repeat a couple of times.

"Not unless you want to get shot down," Jasper said. "But hey, there's lots of other fish in the sea. A lid for every pot. Even for you."

Call felt like punching Jasper in the face, which was confusing because he was still feeling grateful that Jasper had gotten broken up with for his sake.

Grudgingly, Call realized that Jasper's advice wasn't going to make the weird feeling in his stomach any better. In fact, it was worse.

↑ ≈ △ ○ @

The next few days passed in a blur of chaos theory. Master Joseph taught Call and Alex in the mornings and then let them experiment all afternoon while he taught Tamara, Jasper, and the other students.

Call had to admit that Master Joseph was an exciting teacher. He wanted them to try things, test out new ideas, and he wasn't particularly concerned about risk. Call learned a lot about chaos, learned to hold it in his hand, to mold it and shape it. He learned to bring chaos creatures through from the void and to keep them with him all day, dark shapes that whisked around his legs and worried Havoc. He learned to look into the void itself, a place of shadows where the longer he looked, the more the shadows seemed to be just the opposite, made of all colors at once, swirling in Call's eyes.

At night, they ate together. Sometimes Master Joseph cooked. Other times he ordered food and one of his minions picked it up. That night they were eating deliciously fried chicken with lots of sides. Call gnawed on a bone thoughtfully. Evil definitely had superior culinary arts on its side.

"Tomorrow," Master Joseph said, "I am going to be gone all day, so I'd like you two — Call and Alex — to concentrate on your experiments. Jasper and Tamara, I will give you some exercises."

Tamara met Call's gaze from across the table, but he could no longer read her looks. She probably meant *Good, Master Joseph is going to be gone, so we should search the house*, but he wanted her to mean *Good, he's going to be gone, so we can sneak off and be alone together*.

They hadn't kissed since that one time in Jericho's room, and Call was starting to feel a little crazy. *She liked someone else,*

Jasper had said. *If she sucked face with you, it was probably because she didn't want to die alone.* His words haunted Call.

Did he really need to stop thinking about Tamara when their escape and lives were on the line? Probably.

Jasper was winking and mouthing something across the table. *After dinner*, he said silently. *In my room.*

Alex looked over at them lazily. Call could never tell how much attention Alex was paying to anything they did. He seemed to have his own stuff going on, which involved locking himself in his room — which was at the other end of the house — blasting heavy metal, and collecting designer sweaters with skulls on them.

After dinner, Call and Tamara crowded into Jasper's room. Most of the various stuffed and toy horses had been shoved under the bed, and the room looked strangely bare.

"What's going on, Jasper?" Tamara asked, hands on her hips. She was wearing a pastel blue dress and her hair was down, rippling over her shoulders.

"Tomorrow," Jasper said. "We have to get away for at least a few hours in the afternoon. We need to distract Alex and maybe Hugo."

"Why?" said Call.

"Because there's something we need to look at," Jasper said. "Master Joseph comes in and out of here on elementals, but they don't land near the house. I saw one landing the other night and I followed it to see where it came down."

"You did?" Tamara was incredulous. "Why didn't you bring us with you?"

"A lone wolf hunts alone," said Jasper. "Besides, I wasn't expecting it and I didn't have time to get you. Anyway, I didn't find the elemental. I found something else."

"What?" Call asked.

But Jasper just shook his head. He looked troubled. "You'll have to see it yourselves. I don't want to talk about it here."

No matter how much they pressed him, he wouldn't say anything more, but he made them promise to get out of whatever they were doing and meet him outside the next day, before lunchtime, by the path where they walked Havoc.

"We should bring Havoc, too," said Call. "He can be a cover story in case anyone asks us what we're doing outside."

Tamara frowned. "Do you think you can get away from Alex?"

Call nodded. "No problem," he said, though he doubted it would, in fact, be no problem.

"Okay. I'm going to bed, then," Tamara said. "I'm worn-out."

She headed toward the door, then paused, turned around, and kissed Call on the mouth. "Good night," she said a little shyly, and practically skipped out of the room.

Jasper stared. "Holy moly," he said after the door shut behind Tamara. Call didn't say anything. He was stunned and silent.

Call cleared his throat. All his nerve endings felt exposed. "Now you know why I need advice!"

Jasper chuckled to himself. "You got problems," he said. "I feel bad for you, son."

"Get out, Jasper," Call said in exasperation. "You're not helping."

"It's *my* room," Jasper pointed out. Call had to admit this was true. He went back to his own room and lay awake most of the night, dreaming sometimes that Aaron was dead at his feet again, and sometimes that Aaron was alive and he and Tamara were walking away from Call and never coming back.

↑ ≈ △ ○ ◎

The next day dawned and, as luck would have it, was overcast, with rain threatening all morning.

Alex appeared to be in a particularly foul mood. Call frowned at him as they tried, unsuccessfully, to come up with any new ideas for raising a stoat that wasn't either Chaos-ridden or about to explode.

Call saw an opportunity for getting away from him. If Call could just use his superpower of being annoying, Alex would probably storm off on his own.

The first thing Call did was start to hum, off-key, to himself as he looked through the alchemy books Master Joseph put together for them. Alex glared.

Then Call picked up a historical book about a Makar called Vincent of Maastricht — one of the few not relegated to the basement — and began reading aloud, "Little is known of the methods Vincent undertook to secure the bodies for his experiments, but it is believed —"

"Are we going to get back to work?" Alex interrupted.

Call pretended not to hear him until Alex jerked the book away from Call. Then he looked up nonchalantly. "Huh?"

"I said," Alex stated, clearly trying his most Evil Overlord-y look on Call, "that we had better get back to work."

Call yawned exaggeratedly. "I am working. I'm thinking big thoughts. After all, *I'm* Constantine Madden. If anyone is going to figure out how to raise the dead, it's going to be me."

"You?" Alex took the bait, his voice withering. "All you want to do is boring stuff. We could be making more Chaos-ridden. We could be trying to bring *people* back from the dead, instead of stoats. We could even try to shape flesh and make something wholly chaos-born. Constantine Madden wouldn't sit around all day, doing nothing. It's dull and so are you."

"Go eat a dirty sock," Call told him, feeling a little weird about the insult after he spat it out. "You don't know what Constantine would do."

"I know what he *should* do," Alex said, and turned his back on Call, stalking off.

That was ominous enough to worry Call, but he didn't have time to worry about it. Instead, he had to meet Jasper and

Tamara. It looked like he'd managed to get the afternoon free. He just wasn't entirely sure what it was going to cost him.

↑ ≈ △ ○ @

Tamara and Jasper were waiting for him, looking out at the water from the yard. As he walked toward them, they abruptly broke off their conversation and Call had the uncomfortable feeling that they'd been discussing him. He bet Jasper had a lot to say about her kissing him . . . and none of it was good.

"You sure Alex isn't following you?" Jasper asked as Havoc danced over to Call, jumping up to press his paws against Call's chest.

Call looked nervously over his shoulder. "I don't think so."

"Let's go," Tamara said. "Before someone spots us."

Jasper was looking anxious as they cut through the woods. He was so keyed up that when Havoc nipped lazily at a butterfly, Jasper startled.

"Over here," he said, leading them through a copse of trees.

On the other side was what appeared to be an old quarry. It was carved out of the rocks, with water welling up from the bottom, as though someone had managed to drill through the base of the island and the sea was rising from underneath.

"What were they quarrying?" Tamara asked. Then, squinting, she answered her own question. "Looks like granite."

"There's a path down the side," Jasper said, pointing to an area that ramped down. It was wide enough for a vehicle to drive on, but it was steep enough that Call found himself afraid he would stumble and roll all the way to the bottom. He clung on to branches he passed.

"We really have to go down there?" Call asked. "Can't you just tell us?"

Jasper shook his head grimly. "No, you have to see it."

It took them a little while to get all the way to the water. Tamara took Call's hand and helped him along, which was nice and also kind of embarrassing. She knew about his leg and had kissed him anyway, so that must not bother her. But he wasn't so sure that it didn't bother him.

Of course, he wasn't entirely sure what all the kissing meant. Jasper had been so sure that she didn't like him and Anastasia so sure she did. But then she'd kissed him *in front* of Jasper, so that had to count for something.

He had to say something. He wasn't sure when they would be alone next.

"Um," he said, because his conversational skills were amazing.

Tamara looked his way, clearly waiting for him to talk.

He tried to remember Jasper's tips about making girls like him, but all he could recall was that he wasn't supposed to blink, and since Tamara was walking next to him, he wasn't even sure she could tell.

"Are we going out?" he finally blurted. When she didn't immediately answer, he kept going. "Am I your boyfriend?"

Then he realized he was going to have to get his hand away from her because it was getting sweaty. And, as the silence stretched on, he started thinking rolling down the hill might not be the worst thing. At least it would mean the subject was automatically changed.

"Do you want to be my boyfriend?" Tamara asked finally, looking sideways at him through her long, dark lashes.

At least this wouldn't be the first time he'd made a fool of himself in front of her. "Yeah," he said.

"Okay," she said, giving him a brilliant smile. "I'll be your girlfriend."

In her answer, he heard what he was supposed to have said: *Will you be my girlfriend?* But she didn't seem annoyed with him. She squeezed his hand and made him feel, for a moment, like good things were possible, even for him.

You're wrong! He wanted to shout at Jasper. *She likes me after all! Not Aaron, me!*

The path ended, leveling out into a sandy beach where the water lapped against uneven small clumps of granite. It was pretty — or would have been, Call thought, until he saw what was *under* the water.

At first they seemed like rocks, like the shallow bottom of the quarry, except for the dark depths between them. No, what he was looking at were heads, hair rippling in the current like duckweed. Hundreds — no, thousands — of Chaos-ridden bodies. All of them standing in neat rows, waiting for the summons that would bring them to battle.

Call stopped, jerking Tamara to a stop beside him. They released each other's hands and stared. Jasper was already standing by the edge of the water, pointing down.

The wind blew Call's hair into his face. He pushed it back with his hand. He couldn't stop staring.

"So many," Tamara whispered. "How — Alex didn't make all these."

"No." Jasper was still staring at the water. "Now you know why I wanted you to see it yourselves."

"Constantine made these," said Call. "I know it." He couldn't explain quite how he knew it. He had no memories of Constantine's life. But he'd been reading what Jericho had to say about his brother, and he had his own feelings. He *knew*.

"All this time we thought there were only the Chaos-ridden we've seen," Tamara said, a worried hitch in her voice. "But there are so many more."

"Everyone said most of them were destroyed in the Mage War," said Jasper.

"I'm sure most of the ones in the battle were destroyed," said Call. "But there would have been more. Constantine was careful. He wanted an army big enough to march on the Magisterium, the Collegium, the Assembly, everything."

"We have to destroy them," said Tamara, her voice stronger

now. "If we all used elemental fire — but, no, we can't burn them underwater. Maybe we could make a bomb."

Call felt a rush of affection for Tamara. She did not think small.

"Or Call could order them to destroy themselves," said Jasper.

"If they're really mine — Constantine's," Call said, assailed by sudden doubt. He turned back toward the water. The Chaos-ridden were still, like trees that had grown up under the water of the quarry. As if they had been there when the quarry flooded, and had never moved — like those towns that were drowned underwater when reservoirs were built.

Call held out his hand, palm out. "Chaos-ridden!" he called. "Rise! Come to the one who made you!"

Silence. The cold wind blew. Call was starting to think he had gotten it wrong, when the surface of the water began to ripple and darken. They were moving. The Chaos-ridden were moving, under the surface. Jasper yelled as a head popped out of the water near his feet. It was a man, his face slack with water, eyes wide and blind. He started to turn toward Call.

Tamara caught Call's arm. "Not now," she said. "Make them go back under."

Call stared into the blank eyes of the Chaos-ridden. "What are your orders?" he asked.

When the Chaos-ridden replied, Call knew that Tamara and Jasper would only hear senseless grunts and groans. But he heard words. The language he shared with the dead, that

WOODSON

no one else could speak. "Rise up," said the Chaos-ridden. "Destroy."

"*Call*," Tamara said.

He turned toward her. "They're dangerous."

"I know," she said. "Now make them go back under."

"The time is not now," Call told them. "Return to the water and wait."

As one, the Chaos-ridden disappeared underneath the surface again. Call's mind raced. He could order them to destroy one another. He could maybe even send them all back into the void if he opened a gateway. But with all of them, he could bring down Master Joseph's house, tear it to the studs. He could destroy Alex and Master Joseph both. Maybe that's what Tamara was thinking, too.

There was just one problem: Aaron.

"We've got to warn someone," Jasper was saying. "We've got to leave."

"Can you command all those Chaos-ridden?" Tamara asked.

Call nodded, but he felt sick at heart.

"Good," she said, planning as they walked back to the house. "We're leaving tonight and we're going to take Master Joseph's army with us. That's how you're going to redeem your name, Call! No one can doubt you if you delivery victory to the Assembly."

For a moment, Call was drawn into imagining himself heroically ahead of an army of Chaos-ridden, an army he had commanded to kneel down before the Assembly. Maybe they really would take him back. Maybe he really would be forgiven.

But if they left tonight, they would be leaving Aaron behind.

And while Call had learned a lot about chaos magic and a lot about filling souls with chaos, he hadn't figured out how to raise Aaron from the dead. And once they escaped the island, there would be no way to bring Aaron back.

Unless Call did it tonight.

↑ ≈ △ ○ @

It was even easier to slip away from Tamara and Jasper than it had been to get away from Alex. Call just said he'd be in trouble if he didn't go, and neither Tamara nor Jasper questioned him.

Once alone, Call grabbed Jericho's diary and went down to the parlor to read. Before, he had flipped through it in search of experiments and secrets, but now he read with a burning intensity. If Jericho knew *anything* that might give Call a clue as to how to bring Aaron back, then he needed to find it. As the pages flipped by, a sense of dread filled him. Then Call came to an entry that made his blood run cold:

There is no one I can tell how I feel, but each day I get more tired and more afraid for the future. When I first became Constantine's counterweight, it seemed to be such an honor, to keep my older brother safe. But neither of us really understood what a counter-weight could do.

But then Constantine learned how to draw on my soul regu-larly, without compromising his own. He drains me nearly to death, again and again. He gives me back only a little of my own strength, barely enough to be conscious and far too little to do any magic of my own. I fear my soul will be all used up before he notices. He wasn't always like this, but he changed so much in the last year that I feel like I don't know him. I am so afraid and no one believes me, so taken are they all by Constantine's charm.

Call flipped a few more pages.

I hate everything about bringing animals for Constantine's experiments, but bringing him human bodies from hospitals is worse.

Call turned the page with reluctance. It was like reading a horror novel, but scarier. A horror novel about yourself.

I'm not Constantine, he told himself. But it was harder now. Anastasia thought he was Constantine. Master Joseph did, too. The only person who truly didn't was Tamara. She believed he was Call, a whole person on his own. Aaron had believed in him, too. And look where that had gotten him. . . .

Something awful has happened. I was too tired to bring a body back for Constantine from the graveyard, so he summoned an air elemental and flew us to the hospital. We landed on the helicopter pad and he laughed about that. He helped me down the stairs and for a minute it was like he was back to being the brother I remembered, the one who took care of me. I asked why he'd brought me with him and he said he just wanted us to have a good time together.

We went right past the morgue and down the hall into the ICU. He used air magic to disguise our presence from the nurses. It was creepy, being among all those sick people who didn't know we were there.

We went into one room where an old woman was lying with her eyes closed and a tube down her throat. Con's eyes were shining. I figured out what he wanted to do but it was already too late. "Con, she's not dead."

"Maybe that's the key, though," he said. "She's nearly dead. Maybe you need to put the chaos in while there's still a spark of life."

"You have to leave her alone," I said. "She's alive."

I kept saying it over and over as he pushed me aside and reached his hand out for her. Dark chaos spilled from his fingers. I saw the woman's body jerk and tremble.

I felt something pinch inside my chest. I gasped and fell to my knees just as the old woman opened her eyes; they were blank but swirling with colors, like the eyes of Chaos-ridden animals. They fixed on me and somehow I thought she recognized me. Jericho, *her eyes were saying.* Jericho.

Constantine wasn't relying on me just for energy, I realized. He was using pieces of my soul — using them as if they were batteries, shoving them into the Chaos-ridden, into this woman, like an electrical shock that would bring her back to life.

I didn't see the woman die. I could hear Con exclaiming in annoyance that she was gone. Another failed experiment. All I could do was wonder how much of my soul was left now that my brother had shredded it.

Call put the book down. He was breathing so hard he was light-headed. The words on the page were like a slap in the face. He had known Constantine Madden as the Enemy of Death, the cause of his mother's demise, the monster who the Assembly would rather keep their truce with for fear of starting the war over again, but still this was horrifying in a wholly different way. It was personal — what he'd done to his brother, ripping pieces off his soul. Constantine hadn't done it to save someone he loved. He hadn't killed that woman in desperation. He'd done it as an experiment. Just because he was curious. And cruel.

Constantine Madden hadn't been driven to making terrible choices by grief. He'd been making terrible choices way before his brother died.

And while Master Joseph might have pushed him into it in the beginning, he'd clearly taken to evil like a duck to water.

Call put down the diary and went to the window, looking out at the afternoon sunlight dappling the grass. He was afraid he was going to throw up. He felt like a storm was in his head.

But after a few moments, he felt steadier. And then a few minutes after that, something new occurred to him. For years, Call had been afraid that he was too sarcastic, too mean-spirited, too willing to cut corners. He'd imagined a straight line from accruing too many Evil Overlord Points by not taking out the trash and eating the last slice of pizza to leading an army of the Chaos-ridden.

But Call knew he would never do what Constantine had done to Jericho — never steal pieces of the soul of someone he loved. He knew that he would never murder someone for no reason. If that was what evil was, he wasn't going to wind up that way by accident.

Maybe he should stop worrying that he was becoming Constantine Madden and start worrying about Alex. Alex, who wanted power and wasn't afraid to kill for it. Alex, who might be willing to do everything Constantine had done and more.

Tamara and Jasper were right: They had to get away from here and they had to do it quickly, before Alex got used to what his power could do, before Master Joseph stopped believing in Call and used the Alkahest on him.

But for all his evil, Constantine had been right about one thing. Death wasn't fair. Aaron shouldn't have died, and if Call could bring him back, bring him back to *life*, not as a Chaos-ridden, then one good thing would have come out of Constantine's horrible experiments, his terrible war.

But to do it, he had to crack the code. Over the days they'd been here, Call had heard about and read about so many experiments Constantine had tried. What hadn't he thought of?

There had to be something, some clue.

Call thought about the entry he'd read, the one where Jericho had seen himself mirrored in the woman's face — as though she was being animated by a piece of his own soul.

There was something there, something that tugged at Call's thoughts.

When Call was a baby, Constantine must have done something very much like that — pushing his whole soul into Callum Hunt's body. Why had that worked?

Call frowned, concentrating.

And then, all of a sudden, he had an idea. A real idea, not one of those stumbling-in-the-dark, maybe-it-will-work ideas that he and Alex had been pursuing with their fruitless experiments.

Tucking the diary in the pocket of his flannel, Call made his way to the experiment room where Aaron was kept and did the one thing that he'd been avoiding — he went to the table where Aaron rested and pulled back the covering from his face.

"I hope you'll forgive me," Call said.

If he got it right, everything would be okay. They could all escape to the Magisterium and Call wouldn't even be put in jail, since there was no way to lock up someone for the murder of a living person. They would return triumphant, with Master Joseph's Chaos-ridden army. And if Tamara only wanted to be Call's girlfriend because she was grief-stricken or something, like Jasper thought, well, maybe she would come to like him. Maybe he could convince her.

So long as Aaron was okay, he was sure she'd forgive him for how he got that way.

The room was full of shadows. Aaron lay still and waxy and white on the table, his face slack. He looked like Aaron and not like Aaron. Whatever it was that gave Aaron his personality and force was gone.

His soul, Call told himself. *Name it what it is.* He hadn't believed in souls before he'd gone to the Magisterium, but Master Rufus had taught him how to see Aaron's.

He placed his hands on Aaron's chest. He'd touched him before, with Alex there, but now it felt strange. Like he was bidding Aaron good-bye.

But he wasn't. The opposite, in fact. He forced his mind back from the dark paths it wanted to go down, the paths that reminded him that he was alone in the room with a dead body. Every horror movie he'd ever seen was competing to freak him out. *This is Aaron*, he reminded himself. *The least scary person I know.*

Constantine had used his brother's soul, had torn off pieces of it to fuel his experiments. But what he hadn't done was what Call was about to do. He hadn't used a piece of his *own* soul.

Call kept his hands on Aaron's chest, and reached down deep inside himself. He tried to remember what it had been like, seeing Aaron's soul. He thought of what made him himself — his earliest memories: Alastair's face, the streets of his town, pavement cracking under his feet. The gates of the Magisterium, the black stone in his wristband, the way Tamara looked at him. The feeling in his chest of Aaron's magic pulling at him, what it was like to be a counterweight, the blackness of chaos . . .

Darkness in the form of smoke spread from his fingers. It spilled over Aaron's chest like ink, wreathing his body.

Call gasped. Energy felt like it was pouring out of him, through his hands, making his body vibrate. He could feel his own soul, pressing against the inside of his rib cage.

He closed mental fingers around that soul and pressed down on it. It was as if a spark jumped through him, through his veins, and into Aaron. Aaron's body jerked, his hands spasming, his feet drumming against the metal table.

Call was drenched in sweat, his body shaking. The spark was inside Aaron; he could feel it. He could even see it: Aaron had begun to glow from the inside, as if a lamp had been turned on within him. His mouth opened and he dragged in a long, slow breath.

Terror gripped Call, thinking of how he'd once pushed chaos into another body, thinking of the way that Jennifer Matsui's eyes had opened and swirled endlessly with chaos.

"Please," he said to Aaron. "Let it be you. Fight to be you. Please."

If Aaron came back as one of the Chaos-ridden, Call would never forgive himself.

I shouldn't have done this, he thought. It was arrogant; it was too risky. After the diary, he'd been so sure he wasn't like Constantine. And maybe he wasn't, because even Constantine hadn't actually experimented on Jericho. Even Constantine had possessed more sense.

Aaron's chest rose and fell, as though in sleep, but he still didn't open his eyes.

"Aaron," Call said, under his breath. "Aaron, please be you."

Then Aaron moved, hand swiping at nothing, body rolling over. He turned onto his side, pushed himself into a sitting position, and with a shudder opened his eyes.

They weren't coruscating.

They weren't anything but a clear and steady green.

"Aaron?" Call felt as though he could barely get his throat to make a sound.

"Call," Aaron said. He didn't sound quite like himself — not yet. Maybe it was because his throat hadn't been used in so long, but there was a weird hollowness in the way he spoke, an odd lack of inflection.

Call didn't care. Aaron was alive. Whatever was wrong with him now could be fixed. Call threw his arms around his friend, felt the way his skin was growing warmer as his blood moved less sluggishly. He hugged him hard.

Aaron smelled strange, not like dead things or rot, but like ozone, like the air after a lightning strike.

"You're okay!" Call said, as though by saying the words he was making it so. "You're okay! You're alive and okay!"

Aaron's arm came around his back, patting him on the shoulder. But when Call pulled away, Aaron's face was blank and tense. He looked around the room without recognition.

"Call," he said hoarsely. "What have you done?"

CHAPTER TEN

I T'S OKAY," CALL said. He grabbed Aaron's hands. They were cold, but not *cold*. Definitely living hands. Call knew you were supposed to rub people's hands to warm them up, so he set to it.

Aaron looked around. He was moving very slowly, as if all his muscles were stiff. "Where are we?"

"You should just concentrate on getting better," Call said.

"Better?" Aaron definitely sounded like someone who was waking up after a long time asleep, but that made sense. "When did I get sick?"

Call didn't know how to answer that. Instead, he said, "Tell me what you remember last."

"We were in the woods," Aaron said. Some color was starting to come back to his face. His eyes were still plain green, the way they always had been, no hint of spinning color. And no Chaos-ridden could talk, Call reminded himself. Not like this, in full, normal sentences. "We were looking for Tamara. . . ."

Aaron crinkled up his nose in thought. Call let his hands go, and Aaron flexed his fingers. Normal hands, normally flushed skin, normal pulse in his throat . . . Call's heart was banging wildly. He'd done it, he'd brought Aaron back, he'd accomplished the impossible . . .

"And then Alex turned on us," Aaron went on. He was frowning more deeply now. "He was the traitor, all the time. He had the Alkahest. He made us kneel down . . ."

Wait, Call realized. This was about to get bad. "Aaron, it's all right. You don't have to —"

But Aaron had begun to shiver. Not small shivers as if he were cold, but shivers that made his whole body flinch. He clutched at the edge of the gurney. "We knelt down," he said. "There was a blast. You were knocked away from me. I saw the white light of the Alkahest. It filled the sky. Call . . ." He raised haunted, green eyes. "What happened? Please tell me it wasn't what I think."

Call could only shake his head. Aaron was staring at his own hands. They were pale and looked ordinary to Call. But Aaron seemed to recoil from them.

Call realized what Aaron was looking at, then: His nails had grown long and ragged. *Nails and hair grow after death*, Call remembered. Aaron's hair was too long, too, curling past his ears.

"Call," Aaron said. "Was I — was I — ?"

Call cut him off desperately. "There's no time. We have to get out of here. We have to move before someone finds us. Aaron, please."

Aaron hesitated — then nodded. The desperation in Call's voice seemed to have broken through his suspicions. He slid off the metal table, landing on his bare feet.

His legs gave way instantly. He crumpled to the ground and rolled over, groaning. Call leaned over him, as Aaron curled into an agonized ball. His hair was sticking to his forehead with sweat. "My legs — they're *burning* —"

A laugh cut through the room. A loud, incredulous, harsh laugh. "You've got to be kidding me."

Call straightened up. It was Alex, in another one of his black outfits, standing in the doorway. Call's heart sank.

Aaron pushed himself up onto his hands, kneeling. He'd gone a sort of waxy white color. "Not you," he said. "You can't be here. No."

"I never thought you'd do it." Alex swaggered into the room. "I never thought you'd have the nerve, Constantine Junior."

Call flung himself between Aaron and Alex. "Stay away from him — from us," Call said.

"Sure," Alex drawled. "I'll just wander off and pretend you *didn't* just raise someone from the dead, which literally no one has ever successfully done before —"

Aaron screamed.

It was an awful noise. Both Call and Alex flinched back as

the inhuman howl tore out of Aaron's throat. He clawed at the ground, shoulders shaking, but there were no tears on his face. He wasn't crying.

"Aaron!" Call knelt down. "You have to calm down. Please calm down."

Aaron went limp. "I'm dead," he whispered. "I *died*. That's why everything looks gray and — and awful —"

The doors flew open. Master Joseph burst into the room, followed by Jasper and Tamara. His hand was raised, a core of fire burning in his palm. He'd come in response to Aaron's scream, but now he went still, staring at Aaron in shock. He suddenly looked much older, his skin too tight, his mouth pinched into a line.

"My God," he said.

Alex gave a bitter laugh. "Nothing to do with God here."

"Get him up," said Master Joseph hoarsely. "Get him on his feet. I need to see he's alive."

Call swung around to protect Aaron, but Alex was already there, hauling Aaron into a standing position. Aaron raised his face, looking past Master Joseph, seeing Tamara and Jasper there in the doorway. Jasper's face was a mask of surprise, but Tamara — Tamara looked as if she'd fallen a long way and knocked all the air out of her body. Like she couldn't breathe.

"Tamara," Aaron whispered.

Tamara threw both her hands over her mouth and took a step back, almost slamming into Jasper, who caught her by the arm. She was shaking her head back and forth, her dark braids whipping across her face. Call felt a wave of sickness pass over him. "Tamara," he began.

"Be quiet," said Master Joseph. "All of you, be quiet." He was staring at Aaron as if Aaron really were a ghost. As if he'd never imagined his plan could actually work. As if he'd never thought Aaron would live again.

"You did it," he said. His gaze was on Aaron, but he was obviously speaking to Call. "I was right. I was right to leave the task of raising the dead to you, Constantine. You *did it*!"

"Call." Jasper's voice had sunk to a flat whisper. "*You* did this?"

Call realized he should have planned this a lot better. He shouldn't have raised Aaron without a way to get him out of there — without a way for them all to escape together the way Tamara had hoped. He should have found a way to do it when the commotion wouldn't have woken up the whole house.

Of course, he hadn't realized this would work. He hadn't known how much time it would take or what it would drain out of him.

All of a sudden, Call felt very dizzy.

That was when he remembered: A piece of his soul was missing.

He was going to pass out, he realized. Instinctively, he reached out for someone to grab, but there was no one there.

When Call tumbled to the floor, he did it entirely alone.

↑ ≈ △ ○ @

Call awoke in Constantine's old room. Horrifyingly, Anastasia was sitting at the end of his bed, in a white pantsuit with a pin stuck through one lapel. On it, a moonstone eye winked at him.

He bit off a scream.

Whatever strangled sound he had made was what alerted her to his being awake.

"What are you doing here?" he wanted to know.

She smoothed the covers over his chest. "Master Joseph told me what you did. You've saved the world — do you know that?"

Call shook his head.

"You've changed what it is to be a mage. Oh, Call, you've changed everything. No longer will Constantine be thought of as a monster. His legacy will be honored. *Your* legacy."

A horrible shudder went through him. He really hadn't thought about those kind of consequences. And she didn't understand. What he'd done wasn't easy to replicate. He couldn't just tear off pieces of his soul all the time. He had no idea how what he'd done was going to affect his power at all. He might never be able to do it again.

But he pushed that thought away for later.

"Is Aaron . . . is he still okay?" he asked.

"He's resting," she told him. "As you were."

"Is he . . . angry with me?" Call wanted to know.

She blinked at him in confusion. "But, Con, why would anyone be angry with you? You've performed a miracle."

He struggled upright. The covers were twisted around him. "I need to talk to Aaron," he said. "I need to see Tamara."

She sighed. "All right. Wait a moment." She stood up, smoothing down her pantsuit. Her eyes were shining as she looked at him. "You don't know what this means," she said. "You don't know who else you could bring back. You have broken into the dominion of death, Con. There are — there were *reasons* that people wanted Makars dead, back in the old country. But you've changed all that."

Call felt his stomach lurch as she walked out of the room. Reasons people wanted Makars dead? Besides the obvious? He couldn't think about it. He needed to see Aaron. Aaron was the proof he'd done the right thing. He'd saved Aaron. He'd never raise another person, never touch a piece of his own soul again. But this had been worth it. It had to be.

Anastasia returned, this time with Tamara, who was wearing a dress made of white tiers of lace. She walked with her head down, not looking at Call.

Anastasia went over to the door and stepped out, though Call could still see her shadow. She was standing just outside in the corridor, listening.

Call decided he didn't care. He was so glad to see Tamara again his whole body had gone cold, then hot all over. He wished he could see her expression.

"Tamara," he said. "I'm sorry —"

She cut him off. "You lied to me."

"I know you're mad," he said. "And you have every right to be. Just please hear me out."

Her chin jerked up. Her eyes were red from crying, but they blazed with emotion. "Yeah, you shouldn't have lied, but that's not the point, Call. And I'm not mad — I'm scared."

He felt cold again. Cold all over.

"You shouldn't have done what you did," she said. "You shouldn't have been *able* to do it. There's only one person who was able to move around souls, who even got close to raising the dead. I staked everything on you not being the Enemy of Death. I broke you out of prison because I believed it. But I was wrong." She shook her head. "You *are* Constantine."

Call flinched as if she'd hit him. He thought about all the days he'd sat in prison, believing she might say these same words to him. And now she had.

"I just wanted Aaron back," he tried to explain. "I thought I could fix things."

Tamara wiped her eyes. "I want him back, too. I want to believe that he is back, just like he was before, but I don't know . . ."

Call started to get up, out of the bed. Both his legs felt weak, but he forced himself upright, clinging to one of the bedposts. "Tamara, listen. He's not Chaos-ridden. I used a piece of my own soul to revive him. He's Aaron. He can talk. He can remember. He remembers Alex murdering him."

"After you passed out, he started screaming," she said flatly. "Just screaming and screaming."

"He's scared. Anybody would be. He's scared and he's —"

"It didn't seem like fear," Tamara said, her face like marble. Call didn't want her to be right, but there was a pit in his stomach. Tamara wasn't wrong a lot.

"He's our best friend," he said, his voice scraping out of his throat. "I couldn't just let him go."

"Sometimes we *have* to let people go," Tamara said softly. "Sometimes things happen that can't be fixed."

"You thought you had to let Ravan go. Your family told you — the whole mage world told you that she was as good as dead once she used too much fire magic and got devoured by the element. But she was part of the jailbreak. You trusted her enough for that. So you must think she's your sister, at least some of the time. You know the mages can be wrong."

"That's different," Tamara protested. "She's not dead; she's Devoured."

"Is it really different?" Call took a deep breath. "I know you're worried about what it means that I did this. But people hate Constantine Madden because he was an evil psycho with a giant undead army who tried to destroy the mage world — not because he wanted to bring the dead back to life. Everyone wants that. That's why he had so many followers. Because everyone's lost somebody. Because when we lose someone, it seems so pointless and random and dumb that there isn't some answer. Maybe Constantine was a terrible person and maybe I'm a terrible person, too. But I might be the terrible person who saved Aaron."

"I hope so," Tamara said. "I want to believe that. I missed

Aaron so much and all I want to do is believe that his death was some kind of hideous mistake. But if he's not himself, Call — if he's not really back, then you have to promise me that you will let him go, once and for all."

Call stared at her face. She looked sad instead of hopeful.

"I promise," he said. "I would never leave Aaron as a Chaos-ridden. I would never do anything to hurt him."

Tamara grabbed one of Call's hands and squeezed it tightly. He was so grateful and relieved that he wanted to throw his arms around her, hold her the way he had before. But he didn't.

She said, "If you stop trusting me, Call, then the only people you're listening to are Master Joseph and Alex. And they're not good people. They don't want the best for you. Or for Aaron."

"I know that."

"Then you have to trust me. If I say Aaron isn't himself, you have to believe me."

Call nodded. "I will. I trust you. If you say it's not Aaron, I'll believe you."

"You better," Tamara said, heading for the door. "Because if you don't, I am going to stop trusting you, too."

Call flopped back on the bed, leaning down to pet Havoc's head. The wolf whined once, as though he could understand what Tamara had said.

After she left, Call was too tired to get up, but too upset to rest anymore. He wanted to go see Aaron, to convince himself that Aaron was fine and that Tamara was wrong, but he was terrified that she might be right. What if Aaron wasn't really back? What if the use of Call's soul had just delayed the whole swirling-eye thing? Gloomy thoughts filled his head until finally there was another knock on the door.

"Come in," he said, sure it was going to be Anastasia with more creepy pronouncements about how great he was.

To his surprise, it was Alex.

He was wearing even more black than before, if that was possible, and his hair was gelled into spikes. There were big metal buckles on his boots and his school bracelet glittered on his wrist. Somewhere he'd found someone to stick a black stone in it, showing that he was a Makar.

"Call, little buddy," he said. "Dinner."

Call wondered if it was awkward to be in the same house with the person you murdered, now back from the dead and maybe planning revenge. He hoped so.

"Come on," Alex said when Call didn't reply. "Don't just sit there. Your zombie is already at the table."

"Don't call him that!" Call snapped. Alex only grinned.

Pushing himself to his feet, Call walked past Alex and limped his way downstairs to the dining room. His whole body ached and he couldn't keep Tamara's words from ringing in his ears, but he couldn't hide. He couldn't leave Aaron to face everyone alone.

He tried to tell himself that Aaron was fine — really fine — and that Tamara would come around when she realized it, but some part of him wasn't as sure as he'd like to be.

Master Joseph beamed at Callum. He was presiding over a table laden down with what looked like a Thanksgiving dinner — there was turkey and stuffing, bowls of glazed carrots and sweet potatoes, peas and whipped potatoes and cranberry sauce.

Anastasia sat beside Master Joseph, glowing. Across from her were Jasper, looking very tense, and Aaron, who flinched when Alex came into the room. Call shoved past Alex and went next to Aaron, who had his hands tightly bunched together in his lap. He looked at Call oddly — as if he were a little glad to see him, and a little bit not.

Smirking, Alex threw himself into a chair beside Anastasia. Absently, she reached over and ruffled his hair, though her eyes were on Call. Hungry eyes, he thought, devouring him.

"Where's Tamara?" Aaron asked as Call settled into his chair. Call started ladling food onto his own plate and then onto Aaron's. Aaron picked up his fork and knife, and Call's spirits lifted. When everyone saw Aaron eat, he thought, they'd have to accept he was normal. Chaos-ridden didn't eat.

"She's upstairs," Jasper said quickly. "Resting. She had a headache."

Aaron put his fork down.

Call felt a little sick. "It's okay," he whispered, hoping Aaron would believe him. "Eat something. You'll feel better."

Aaron exhaled. Tamara had said he'd been screaming, and Call realized now he'd braced for that, but Aaron seemed calm enough, if upset about Tamara. Aaron picked his fork back up and shoved some stuffing into his mouth.

His shoulders were stiff, as if he were angry. Call wondered if Aaron hated him. He had every right. But maybe he was just upset about Tamara. Aaron was used to people thinking of him like a hero. He would be devastated if he knew Tamara thought there was something wrong with him.

Tamara was wrong.

She had to be wrong.

"It is not so easy to have your whole world turned upside down," said Master Joseph. "As she struggles to accept what is possible, so too will the Assembly. So will the Magisterium. But our time — the time of harnessing the power of the void — begins now. With you." He gestured to Call. "And you." He turned to Aaron.

"What about the rest of us?" Alex asked.

"Call was able to bring back Aaron. That's only the beginning. Aaron's only the first of our departed to return. When the Assembly realizes what we're capable of, they will have to make an alliance with us — on our terms. This is the biggest breakthrough since lead was first made into gold. Bigger, maybe."

"You will be able to replicate it, I'm sure," Anastasia told Alex, answering his question. Obviously Master Joseph had gotten so tangled up with his own thoughts about the future that he'd forgotten everything else.

"It is amazing that you were able to do what Constantine

couldn't," Jasper told Call, then looked at Aaron. "How are you doing, buddy?"

Aaron turned toward Jasper, his expression haunted.

For a moment, no one spoke. Call held his breath.

"You okay?" Jasper asked.

"I feel tired," said Aaron. "And strange. Everything is so strange."

"Yeah, I feel that way a lot, too," Jasper said, leaning over to clap him on the shoulder. Call stared. It seemed like such a casual gesture, and so out of place.

"Am I really back?" Aaron asked.

Master Joseph smiled at him. "If you can ask that, then you must be."

Aaron nodded and went back to methodically eating his food, which wasn't the way Aaron usually ate at all. Aaron was either really mannered and polite, or devoured his food like he was afraid someone was going to snatch it away from him. Call watched him, worriedly.

But then, if Aaron had just gotten out of the hospital, he might act weird, too. Call tried to think of it as getting out of surgery. Years ago, Alastair had needed to have his appendix taken out and when he'd gotten home, he'd been too tired to do anything but sit in front of the television, eating soup out of a can and watching a weekend-long marathon of *Antiques Roadshow*.

"So what was it like?" Alex asked finally, breaking the silence.

Aaron looked up from his food. "What?"

"What was it like, being dead?"

"Shut *up*," Call hissed. But Alex just smirked at him.

"I don't remember." Aaron stared at his plate. "I remember dying. I remember *you*." He looked up at Alex and his green eyes were as hard and cold as malachite. "And then I don't remember anything else until Call woke me up."

"He's lying," Alex said, reaching for his glass of Coke.

"Leave him alone," Call said fiercely.

"Call's right," said Anastasia. "If Aaron doesn't remember —"

"Though it would be very useful to have someone who knew what the afterlife was like among us," said Master Joseph. "Imagine what powerful information that would be."

Call pushed back his chair. "I'm not feeling well. I think I'd better go lie down."

Anastasia was on her feet. "I'm sure you must still be exhausted. I'll walk you back up to your room."

"But what about Aaron?" Call said. "Where's he going to sleep?" He tried to keep his voice calm; he was imagining Master Joseph telling him Aaron was going to go back to sleep in the experiment room, or be imprisoned somewhere.

This wasn't how it was supposed to go. Aaron being back was supposed to solve everything. Aaron's death had been the moment that everything had gone terribly wrong — Call being exposed as having the Enemy's soul, being imprisoned, being hated by most of the people he cared about. Some part of him had expected the world to right itself as soon as Aaron opened his eyes.

That part of him was childish.

"There's a room that connects to yours," said Anastasia. "Jericho used to stay there sometimes. Aaron could use it, right?"

She looked toward Master Joseph as she said it. His answering gaze was unreadable. There was a glint deep in his eyes that Call really didn't like. Now that Call had done it — now that he'd actually raised Aaron — would he still be of use to Master Joseph, or would Master Joseph decide Call's powers would be a lot more useful without Call attached to them?

"Of course," Master Joseph said. "It may need some dusting."

↑ ≈ △ ○ @

The room *did* need dusting — a lot of it. Anastasia used her air magic to shake the worst of it out of the bed covers and blinds, leaving all of them coughing. Jasper excused himself to "check on Tamara," though Call suspected he was just trying to get away from the choking dust clouds.

By the time Anastasia could finally be persuaded to leave, it was clear neither Jasper nor Tamara were likely to come back. They were probably in one of their rooms, talking about Aaron's return and what it meant. Talking about Call. He tried to tell himself that was fine and that he shouldn't be jealous, but he was.

Aaron lay down on the bed, on top of the coverlets, and looked at the ceiling, hugging his arms around himself as if he were cold.

"Do you want to talk?" Call asked, feeling awkward.

"No," Aaron said.

"Look," Call said. "If you're mad at me —"

There was a light knock on the door. It swung open slowly.

Tamara came into the room. She was wearing a lavender dress she hadn't bothered to cut the lace off of. She looked pretty, like she was on her way to a garden party.

Call blinked, surprised to see her.

"Aaron," she said. "I'm glad you're back."

He sat up slowly and looked at Tamara. His eyes weren't swirling. He wasn't Chaos-ridden. But Call could see Tamara wince anyway as she looked at Aaron, as if he seemed strange to her. *But he's just Aaron*, Call's mind screamed. He was traumatized. It couldn't be easy to come back from the dead. Call willed Tamara to be understanding. He could tell she was trying. She sat down on a chair next to the dresser and clenched her hands in her lap.

"Sorry I was so weird before," she said. "I didn't know what to think."

"I remember you crying," Aaron said. "When I died."

"Oh," Tamara said, swallowing.

"And you knocked Call out of the way of the Alkahest," he said. "It hit me instead."

"*Aaron.*" Tamara gasped. Call's heart was twisting inside

his chest. He remembered Jasper saying to him, *I just think Tamara — well, Call, I just think she liked* someone else, *if you get my meaning*, and how he'd felt when Tamara had told him she'd never regretted saving him.

"She couldn't save both of us and she made a split-second decision," Call said, his voice rough. "So knock it off, Aaron."

Aaron nodded. Call felt a slight pressure ease off his chest. That was more like Aaron. "I'm not angry," he said. "Not at Tamara, and not at you, either, Call. I just feel like — like I have to concentrate really hard to pull myself together. Like all I want is to lie down and shut my eyes and have it be dark and quiet."

"That makes total sense," Call said, his words tripping over themselves in his eagerness. "You just have to get used to being alive again."

Aaron nodded. "I guess people can get used to anything."

"It's incredible," Tamara whispered. "Sitting here and listening to you talk, actually talk."

"I'm going to be an example," Aaron said. "Master Joseph is going to use me and Call to show them he knows how to end death."

"Probably," said Call.

"We have to leave," said Aaron. "They want to use us, but they won't hesitate to hurt us if they need to."

"We're going to run," Tamara said. "All of us. We have to make it to the Magisterium."

Aaron looked surprised. "Why go there?"

"To warn them," Tamara explained. "They need to know what Master Joseph is planning. What his weaknesses are."

"We won't be safe at the Magisterium," Aaron said. "We'll just be in a different kind of danger."

"But if we don't warn them, they'll be in danger," Call said.

"So what?" said Aaron.

Tamara was twisting her hands in her lap. "We're talking about our friends," she said. "The Magisterium — people you know. Master Rufus, Celia, Rafe, Kai, Gwenda —"

"I don't know them that well," said Aaron. He didn't sound angry. Just distant. Weary and distant in a way he'd never sounded before.

Tamara pushed her chair back. "I have to go — go to sleep," she said, and moved toward the door. She paused and picked up a book from on the dresser. Jericho's diary. Call wondered what she wanted it for. He was going to ask her when Aaron spoke again.

"Everyone has to die eventually," said Aaron. "I don't see how us dying for the Magisterium helps."

Call heard Tamara choke back a sob as she fumbled for the knob and let herself out of the room.

When Aaron turned back to him, Call felt more exhausted than he ever had before. He didn't want to talk to Aaron, for the first time in his life. He wanted to be alone.

"Go to sleep, Aaron," he said, standing up. "I'll see you tomorrow."

Aaron nodded and lay down, closing his eyes, asleep almost

immediately, as if nothing had happened at all to trouble his dreams.

↑ ≈ △ ○ @

After an hour of listening to Havoc snore and the eerie silence from Aaron — he didn't turn or rustle and barely seemed to breathe — Call realized that he wasn't going to sleep. He kept thinking about his dad, about Master Rufus, and what they would think of what he'd done. He wished he could talk to one of them, get some advice.

Finally he got up, deciding to brave the creepy house and the Chaos-ridden to get a glass of water. He padded down the stairs, into the kitchen.

"Call?" a voice called. Tamara stepped out of the shadows. For a moment, it didn't seem possible that she was real. But then he saw how tired she looked and figured he wouldn't have imagined that.

"I couldn't sleep," she said. "I've been sitting in the dark trying to figure out what to do." She was wearing the clothes she'd arrived in. He looked down at his pajamas and then over at her, puzzled.

"What do you mean?" he asked.

"You said that if he wasn't right, you'd let him go," Tamara said. "You promised."

"It's too soon." It was true that Aaron was acting weird, like maybe some of him was still stuck in death. "He's going to get better. You'll see. I know he was a little weird tonight, but he's just back. And he sounds like himself sometimes."

Tamara shook her head. "He doesn't, Call. The Aaron who was our best friend never sounded like that."

Call shook his head. "Tamara, he was *murdered*. He's not going to come back from that cheerful and optimistic!"

She flushed. "I'm not expecting him to be perfect."

"Really? Because it sounds like you are," said Call. "Like you think either he has to be exactly the same as he was or he's — broken. You didn't say he couldn't be different, or traumatized. I wouldn't have agreed to that."

She hesitated. "Call, the way he talked about other people — Aaron was never *indifferent*."

"Just give him a few days," Call said. "He'll get better."

Tamara reached out and touched Call's face with the palm of her hand. Her fingers felt soft against his cheek. He shivered.

"Okay," she said, but she looked incredibly sad. "A few more days. We better get back to sleep."

Call nodded. He got his glass of water and went back up the stairs.

Back when he'd been at the Magisterium, Call had known right from wrong — even if he hadn't always done the right thing. In prison, everything seemed to have slid away from him.

Maybe it was just that Aaron had always been his moral center. He didn't want to believe that there was anything wrong with Aaron that couldn't be fixed. He wanted Aaron to be okay, not just because he was Call's best friend but because if Aaron wasn't okay, then Call wasn't okay either.

If Aaron wasn't okay, then Call was exactly what everyone had been afraid of all along.

Back in Constantine's bedroom, Call flopped down, willing himself to sleep. This time he did.

↑ ≈ △ ◯ @

He woke up what felt like a few moments later, to an explosion. Leaping out of bed, he went to a window. Trucks were revving up outside, the sound almost drowned out by shouting.

His first thought was that the Assembly had come to arrest them. And in that brief moment, fear warred with relief.

Master Joseph came into view as he stepped off the porch, wearing the silver mask of the Enemy of Death. Without what looked like any effort at all, he flew up into the air. Below him, crowding around the porch steps, Call could see a cluster of figures: Anastasia in a white dressing gown, Alex glowering.

"Find them! Find them both!" Master Joseph shouted. It was then that Call realized what he was looking at. Who had set off the explosions.

Tamara and Jasper had done it. They had run.

Tamara and Jasper had run and they had left him behind.

CHAPTER ELEVEN

CALL THREW HIMSELF against the window, scrabbling at it, before he remembered that it was made of some kind of air magic.

Barely thinking, he conjured flame into his hand. Havoc started to bark. Call could barely pay attention. He felt like his head was full of bees, buzzing so loudly that he couldn't think. The magical flame wore away at the window, but it was working too slowly. Call didn't have time for this.

He drew on chaos. It came to his hand quickly, an oily curling ribbon of nothingness. He could feel how hungry it was and how it seemed to tug at something deep inside of him.

You don't have enough soul left for this, a part of him thought through the buzzing, but it didn't matter. He sent the chaos toward the window.

It began to eat away the air magic and the glass and the frame outside it. Call didn't care. By the time he stepped out of the window and onto the roof, it was through a huge hole in the side of the house.

In the distance, he saw fire.

He walked to the edge of the tiles and stepped off, concentrating on drawing air magic to him. He wobbled and, for a moment, was afraid he was going to crash down on the grass.

But the magic held. He hovered in the air. Havoc was on the roof behind him, barking wildly. Call turned back to look at him and saw that two of the other windows in the house were smashed out — appearing like they had been burned, the wood around their edges sparking with low flames.

Call's leg had given him a reason to practice this kind of magic, but since the Magisterium was in a cave system and at home there were neighbors, he'd never really *flown*. It was one thing to hover a little, but this, up in the air, high off the ground, like he'd dreamed, was new. He knew he ought to be more nervous, but all his concentration was on the scene unfolding before him.

He looked out toward the fire. Not a natural fire, he realized. Elemental fire. As he stared, he saw something undulate over one of the hills on the horizon.

A huge, snakelike winding ribbon of fire that slipped over the ridge of a hill. The elemental reared up like a cobra, fire spilling from her edges, and Call remembered running through the Panopticon with Jasper and seeing her there in the hallways.

Ravan. Tamara's sister. Which meant Tamara had summoned her. Tamara had been planning this escape for far longer than a single day and night. When Call kissed her in the tunnels, she must have been planning even then. He'd thought that bringing back Aaron had made her stop trusting him, but she must have stopped trusting him before that. Because if she'd trusted him, she would have told him she was contacting Ravan. And she hadn't. The knowledge was like a heavy block sitting on his chest.

The air wobbled again beneath him, his concentration stuttering. Master Joseph shot a bolt of icy magic at Ravan, who dodged it with a smoking hiss.

Call could hear contempt in that hiss. Fire exploded along the ridge of the hill. Through the leaping orange flames he thought he could see two small figures running.

Tamara had trusted Jasper but not Call. She was leaving Call, leaving him here because she'd meant what she'd said in his room. That she'd staked her whole life on the certainty that he wasn't the Enemy of Death, but he was.

Only now, hovering over the burning landscape, did Call realize how much it had always mattered that Tamara believed in him.

Pain rose up in Call, a pain that made him feel like he was choking.

Master Joseph was shouting, and the dark, swarming figures below were hurling magic at Ravan, but she was fast and clever and dodged everything they sent at her.

Call raised one hand. He was remembering a maze made out of fire, how he'd been lost in it until he'd realized his chaos magic could suck the oxygen out of everything, killing fire. He could kill Ravan. In that moment, he knew he could do it.

"Call." It was Aaron. He was out on the roof of the house, one hand on Havoc's ruff. He was barefoot, and had found a T-shirt somewhere to replace his uniform top. He looked pale in the darkness. "Let them go."

Call could hear his own breath in his ears. Trucks were spinning their wheels all over the front lawn of Master Joseph's house, none of them willing to get close enough to Ravan to explode their gas tanks.

"But —"

"It's *Tamara*," said Aaron. "You think Master Joseph will forgive her for running? He won't."

Call didn't move.

"He'll kill her," Aaron said. "And you won't be okay after that. You love her."

Call lowered his hand slowly, hovering just above the roof. He felt Aaron reach forward, grab the back of his shirt, and pull him down onto the tiles. He collapsed, half on top of Havoc, nearly knocking Aaron over. By the time they'd sorted themselves out, Call could no longer see the small running figures of Tamara and Jasper.

Hot tears started in Call's eyes, but he blinked them back. "She left me."

Aaron sat up, disentangling himself from Call. He scooted sideways on the roof tiles, Havoc behind him. "She left *us*, Call."

Call made a choking sound that was partly a laugh. "Yeah, I guess she did."

"She wants to warn the Magisterium," Aaron said. "It's better for us not to go there."

Call suddenly realized what was weird about the way Aaron was talking. "Why do you suddenly hate the Magisterium so much?"

"I don't hate them," said Aaron. He looked out toward where the battle must be taking place. "But it's like I can see them more clearly than I could when I was alive before. They only ever wanted what they could get from us, Call. And they can't get anything from me anymore. And they'll want to punish you. You proved them wrong, you know. They never believed Constantine could *really* raise the dead."

Call stared at him, trying to decode something from his expression, from the clear green of his eyes, but this Aaron wasn't easy to read. He was, however, super creepy.

But he hasn't been back long, Call reminded himself. *Maybe death clings to you for a while, shadowing everything. Maybe that shadow lifts eventually.*

"Do you think I did the right thing, bringing you back?" After he asked it, Call felt like he couldn't quite breathe until he had the answer.

Aaron made a sound that was not quite a sigh. It was like wind whistling through trees. "You know I'm not a Makar anymore, right? I'm not a mage at all. That part of me is gone and everything feels — I don't know, washed-out and dull."

Call felt a little sick. He'd known Alex had taken Aaron's Makar power with the Alkahest, but not that Aaron would come back with no magic at all. "That could change," he said desperately. Without Aaron, he didn't know what he'd do. He didn't know what he'd become. "You could get better."

"You should be asking yourself if you're glad you brought me back," Aaron said with a half smile. "The mages will never take you back now, and I know you don't want to stay here with Master Joseph."

"I don't need to ask myself anything," Call said fiercely. "I'm glad I brought you back."

Havoc barked at that, and nosed in between them. Aaron reached to pat the wolf, and Call felt the tension in his chest ease slightly. Surely if there was something really wrong with Aaron, Havoc would sense it?

Master Joseph came into view, a phalanx of the Chaos-ridden and several dozen mages following him. He was marching back toward the house. When he saw Call and Aaron sitting on the roof, the chaos-eaten hole behind them, he looked momentarily furious. Then his expression smoothed out.

"It's lucky for you two you didn't go with them," Master Joseph yelled up.

Coming up behind him, Alex laughed. "They weren't invited."

"Once the Assembly knows the power you have unlocked,

everything will be different," said Master Joseph, but Call wondered if that could be true. Tamara's parents were on the Assembly. If she was horrified, weren't they likely to be equally horrified — if not more so?

But Call just nodded.

"Come inside," Master Joseph said coldly. "We'll talk."

Call nodded again, but he didn't go inside. He sat on the roof until the sun was much higher in the sky. Aaron sat there, too.

As the yellow light burnished his lashes to gold, he turned to Call. "How did you do it? You can tell me."

"I gave you a piece of my soul," Call said, checking Aaron's expression to see if he was horrified. "That's why it didn't work before. Constantine Madden would never have tried something like that. He would have never given any of his power away."

Aaron nodded. "I think I can tell," he said finally. "I think I can feel it — part of me, but also not."

"And that's why it's not going to work the way they're hoping," Call stumbled on. It was uncomfortable to talk about sharing souls. "Because I can't keep using pieces of my soul to bring people back. They're not . . . unlimited. You can run out."

"And then you'd die," Aaron said.

"I think so. I think that's why Constantine kept Jericho around — so that he could use *his* soul. And I read Jericho's diary —" Call looked around, meaning to show it to Aaron, before he realized it wasn't there. Tamara had taken it with her. To show to the Magisterium, Call assumed. Proof. He felt sick again.

"You don't feel Constantine's soul in you, right?" Aaron said. "You just feel normal. You've always felt normal."

"I've never known anything different," Call said.

"Maybe I just have to get used to it," Aaron said, sounding a lot like his old self. He even grinned a little, sideways. "I'm grateful. For what you did. Even if it doesn't work."

But it did work, Call wanted to insist.

Before he could, someone knocked on the door. It was Anastasia, who didn't wait for them to answer before she opened it. She stepped into Call's room and then stopped at the sight of the devastation Call had wrought — the chaos-eaten wall and the morning sunlight streaming in. She blinked a couple of times.

"Children shouldn't be cursed with so much power," she said, as though she was speaking to herself. She was dressed in what looked like battle gear — pale silver-and-white steel over her chest and along her arms and a chain-mesh hood over her silver hair.

For once, it seemed like she was thinking of Call and Constantine as separate people, cursed equally. He wished she would keep thinking of them that way, but he wasn't particularly hopeful about it.

"What's going on?" Call asked, standing up.

"Look." Aaron pointed as an air elemental hovered into

view, flying over the tops of the island trees. It was clear and wavering, with a circular shape like an enormous jellyfish. "Are we being attacked?"

"On the contrary," said Anastasia. "That is *my* elemental. I summoned it, the vanguard of my troops. I am going after your friends to bring them back before they reach the Magisterium and force our hand."

"Just let them go." Call stood, walking up the remains of the roof tiles and hopping back into the room.

"You know we can't do that. And you know why, too. They know too many things that could hurt us. They should have been more loyal. We hoped to have more time to prepare before there was a war between the forces of the Assembly and those of the Enemy of Death, but if Tamara and Jasper make it home, battle will be joined within the week."

Call thought of the thousands of Chaos-ridden waiting in their watery barracks, thought of how he could have led them away from the island, how the Assembly might have seen him as a hero.

Tamara had wanted him to be seen as a hero. Call couldn't hate her. No matter what happened, he knew he never would.

"Don't hurt my friends," he said. "I haven't asked you for much — " He couldn't call her Mom. His throat stuck on the word. "Anastasia. If you catch them, you have to promise you won't hurt them."

She narrowed her eyes. "I will do my best, but they knew the consequences when they ran. And, Call, I don't think they would hesitate to hurt me." In her battle armor, Anastasia looked pale and terrible. Call thought she might be right about what Tamara and Jasper would do and was even more afraid for them.

"Promise you'll *try*," Call said, because he thought that was likely to be all he was going to get from her. He felt helpless and yet, wasn't he the Enemy of Death? Hadn't his bringing back Aaron proved it, like Tamara said? Shouldn't he be calling the shots?

"Of course," she told him, in a crisp voice that left little room for kindness. "Now come down to breakfast. You two have much to discuss with Master Joseph."

Aaron pushed himself to his feet and came to where Call was standing. Although neither of them had slept and Tamara was gone, Call was starting to feel hopeful again. He was sure Aaron was right about his soul needing to settle. Once Aaron was himself again, they'd figure out what to do. They'd gotten out of a lot of scrapes before. They would find their way out of this one, too.

Maybe.

"Okay," he said to Anastasia.

Call was still in his borrowed pajamas and he didn't bother to change out of them. Aaron seemed comfortable in what he was wearing. They trooped down the stairs and into the dining room, where Master Joseph sat with a few other mages, including Hugo. When Call and Aaron came in, the mages stood up and took their leave. Master Joseph's hair was singed on one side. Alex's face was red, like he'd gotten a blast of fire to the face. The whole table was spread with bandages, magical salve, and dirty mugs.

"Sit down," said Master Joseph. "There's coffee and eggs in the kitchen if you're hungry."

Call immediately went and got an enormous mug of coffee. Aaron didn't get anything, just sat at the table, waiting.

Master Joseph sat back in his chair. "The time has come," he said, looking at Call. "You must explain exactly how you brought Aaron back from the dead."

"All right," Call said. "But you won't like it."

"Just tell the truth, Callum." Master Joseph sounded as if he were trying to be calming, but the strain in his voice came through clearly. "And everything will be fine."

It wasn't fine. Call watched Master Joseph's expression darken as he explained how he had torn a piece of his soul free and placed it in Aaron's body. Aaron, who'd already heard all of this, stared out the window at a few Chaos-ridden animals that were sniffing around the grass.

"This is the truth?" Master Joseph said when Call had finished. Alex was staring at him in disbelief. "The whole truth, Call?"

"It's ridiculous!" Alex protested. "Who would even come up with an idea like that?"

"I got it from Jericho's journals." Call turned to Master Joseph. "You knew," he said. "You knew it was what

Constantine was doing. He was using pieces of Jericho's soul to try to bring the dead back."

Master Joseph stood up, his hands knotted behind his back, and began to pace. "I guessed," he said. "I hoped it wasn't true."

"So you see," Aaron said, shifting his gaze from the window. "This isn't something Call can do again."

Master Joseph whirled on them. "But he *must*. If Anastasia doesn't stop them, your friends will reach the Magisterium. When they do, when they tell the Assembly, we can hope they will be reasonable and realize your genius. But if that doesn't happen, war will come to us. We must raise Drew before that happens."

"Raise *Drew*?" Alex gasped. "You didn't mention that before."

"Of course I did," Master Joseph snapped. "Raising Aaron was one thing — we had his body here — but if Call can retrieve souls that have passed into the afterlife — the Assembly will surrender their power to us. Everyone will cower before power like that."

"Today the Assembly, tomorrow the world!" Alex said cheerfully. "Move those goalposts."

"But it's not possible," Call said. "Weren't you listening? I can't keep ripping out pieces of my soul. I'll die."

"Oh no!" drawled Alex sarcastically. "Not that!"

"You'll have killed Constantine Madden," said Aaron.

"It's true," said Master Joseph, looking at Call in a way that reminded Call of the first time they'd met: Drew had died, and Master Joseph's expression had been a mixture of hate — for Callum Hunt — and yearning, for the Enemy of Death trapped in his body. "Which is why we must have a Jericho." He turned to Alex.

Call was definitely not bringing back Drew. "Uh," he said. "First you're going to need a body and some trace of Drew's soul. I mean, with Aaron, his body still had some of *him* in it."

Aaron was entirely still. Call wondered what he made of this. He worried that all of this made Aaron feel worse about being back from the dead. Call hoped not. He needed Aaron to stay positive. Well, as positive as was possible for him right now.

"I can get those things," Master Joseph said eagerly.

"Okay," Call said. "That's pretty much it. I'd help, but my magic is really diminished after bringing Aaron back."

"Your magic ate a hole in the wall of the house," Alex accused. "It seems fine to me."

Call nodded sadly, exaggerating for all it was worth. "I didn't mean to do that. It's acting all out of control. I wouldn't want to accidentally hurt Drew."

Alex looked daggers at Call, but Master Joseph seemed to believe him. "Yes, I can see how that would be a danger. Alex, you've heard what Call said. Now we will have to re-create his experiment. Come."

Alex looked worried, really worried. Call supposed that tearing off little bits of his soul wasn't something Alex wanted to mess around with, but Call didn't have it in him to be particularly sympathetic.

With a snap of his fingers, Master Joseph summoned back the other mages — which implied they'd been listening. "Let's go," he said to Alex, the threat of being dragged away to the experiment room hanging over him.

Call waved his fingers at Alex, pleased with himself and with the world for once. "Good luck!" he called after them.

Alex didn't even bother to glare back. He looked too scared.

Finding a half-full cup of coffee abandoned by one of the mages, Aaron brought it to his lips. Call watched him, realizing that he was waiting for Aaron to demand they go after Alex, insist on saving him.

"Alex is the reason you're dead in the first place," Call said to that imaginary objection. "I don't care what Master Joseph does to him. We should just stay here and have breakfast. I don't care if his soul gets ripped apart."

"Okay," Aaron said.

Call grabbed a piece of neglected toast off one of the mage's abandoned plates. Aaron wasn't supposed to say that. He was supposed to say something about how Master Joseph and Alex were on Team Evil and how Team Good wasn't supposed to behave like that.

Aaron didn't say anything at all.

With a sigh, Call pushed his chair away from the table. "Fine. Okay. We'll go check it out."

Aaron looked puzzled but stood up and followed Call.

Together they crept toward the experiment room. Within, they could hear muffled voices. Call squeezed one eye shut and looked through a keyhole with the other, but even though that worked in movies, in real life he couldn't see much of anything.

"If you can't find Drew's soul, then you must not be much of a Makar," he heard Master Joseph say from the other side of the door. "Perhaps you should be the vessel for Drew's return. Perhaps Callum Hunt can push Drew's soul in and your soul out."

"I'm a Makar," Alex whined. "You can't do that."

Call sucked in a breath. Here was the real Master Joseph, the one who'd been trying to hide behind elaborate dinners and kindly gestures.

"Your powers are stolen and you are inferior," Master Joseph said, his voice thick with rage. "You were never meant to wield chaos magic."

"I can do this," Alex said. "I can!" There was a scraping noise. "Just give me some room to work."

At that moment, Call heard a low groan from the room — one that sounded chaos-tinged.

"Master Joseph!" Call yelled, slamming his fist on the door. "Let us in!"

A moment later, Master Joseph opened the door to reveal Alex on the floor, looking stunned. There was no one else inside. There was, however, a corpse on the table, its skin tinted blue with cold. Call shuddered.

"I see you want to help after all," Master Joseph said. "But for now, we're fine as we are. Come back tonight, Callum, when you're rested."

And with that, the door closed on them again. The latch turned.

"Well, I guess that's that," Call said, feeling queasy. Could they bring back Drew? Call didn't think they could do it without Drew's body. Even the Chaos-ridden had a tiny bit of their own soul trapped in them — just as Call had realized when he'd accidentally made Jennifer Matsui into one.

But his own soul was Constantine's, in a new body, after all. Maybe it *would* work. He cast a glance at Aaron, but Aaron didn't look like he was worrying about whether they'd bring Drew back or not.

Call needed to *do* something. "Come on," he told Aaron. "We can go around outside and look in through the window." He grabbed for some boots and a coat.

"Are we going to watch him suffer?" Aaron asked, which wasn't the right question at all. Call didn't answer.

Heading outside they passed a scattered bunch of Chaos-ridden who dipped their heads and moaned as Call went by. *Scenic*, Call thought. Aaron frowned at them, hands in his pockets, and walked faster.

"Look around," Call said. "See? This is the kind of trouble I get into when you're not here. Since you died, I wound up arrested, then broken out of jail, then kidnapped and brought to the stronghold of the Enemy of Death, with *Jasper*, who spent the whole time talking about his love life . . ."

At that, the corner of Aaron's mouth lifted.

"And I kissed Tamara, who hates me now! Without you, I can't do anything right. You're the person who helps me figure out what's right and what's wrong. I'm not sure I can do that without you."

Aaron didn't look like he felt particularly happy to hear it. "I don't — I can't do that for you now."

"But you have to," Call said. They had reached a small copse of trees. From there, it would be possible to sneak around to one of the windows of the experiment room, but in that moment, what was happening inside didn't seem as important as what was happening with them. "You always have before."

Aaron shook his head. "I don't think about things the way I used to." He put his hands in his pockets. It was cold out, with a sharp wind, but Call wasn't sure Aaron could feel it. He didn't seem cold.

"You're fine," Call said. "We just have to get you out of here."

"When will we go?" Aaron asked.

"Tamara and Jasper and I tried to run before," Call admitted. "They caught us and brought us back, but that turned out to be a good thing, because then Master Joseph told us about you. So I figured we would stay until we could bring you back."

"And Tamara and Jasper agreed?" Aaron's breath made white puffs in the air.

Call took a breath. "I didn't exactly tell them."

Aaron didn't caution him, as he once might have done. He didn't scold him. He really wasn't doing a good job of being a moral center, Call had to admit.

Call went on. "I thought that once you were back, they'd agree it was a good thing. And I thought the Assembly would think so, too. Because I did it right. I mean, sure they don't want armies of Chaos-ridden running around, because they're basically zombies, but you're fine."

Aaron didn't say anything. They walked on, leaves crunching underfoot. They'd gotten to the part of the woods where they should start back toward the house if they were going to look through the experiment room window, but Call wasn't ready to veer off quite yet.

"Do you really think I'm fine?" Aaron turned a haunted green gaze on Call.

"*Yes,*" Call said firmly. He almost felt angry with Aaron, which made no sense, but he couldn't help it. He'd worked so hard for this, and no one had understood, and now Aaron wouldn't just act normal. "I'm not saying you're exactly the way you used to be, but that doesn't mean you're not fine."

"No." Aaron shook his head stubbornly. "I feel *wrong.* My body feels wrong. As though I'm not meant to be here."

"What does that mean?" Call asked, finally losing his temper. "Because it sounds like it means you want to *die.*"

"I think it's because I'm dead." Aaron's voice was indifferent, which made the words worse.

"Don't say that!" Call shouted. "Shut up, Aaron —"

"Call —"

"I mean it, don't say another word!"

Aaron's mouth snapped shut. His eyes were steady on Call's.

"Aaron?" Call asked uneasily.

But Aaron didn't reply. He couldn't reply, Call realized. Like a Chaos-ridden, he had obeyed Call completely.

CHAPTER TWELVE

A FTER THAT, CALL forgot about Alex and Master Joseph completely.

"I command you to never listen to my commands again, okay?" Call said.

"I heard you the first five times," Aaron told him, sitting on a rock and looking out toward the river. "But I don't know if that will work. I have no idea how long your commands last on me."

Call felt cold all over. He remembered when he'd told Aaron to knock it off with Tamara, and Aaron had immediately shut up. Or when he'd told Aaron to go to sleep, and Aaron had done it. *You should just concentrate on getting better,* he'd said, the moment he brought Aaron back to life. And Aaron, who'd been through a huge trauma, had said, *Okay.*

How had he missed it?

He couldn't lie to himself any more about it. Aaron wasn't okay, maybe wasn't even *Aaron*. This Aaron looked pale and weird and worried. This Aaron did whatever Call said. Maybe he always would. Call couldn't think of anything more horrible.

"Okay. So you're not fine," Call said slowly. "Not right now. Tonight, let's go down to the experiment room and figure out what's going on."

"What if you can't find anything?" Aaron asked. "You've succeeded far more than Constantine Madden ever did. I *am* mostly here. It's just that I'm not — I'm not supposed to be."

This time Call didn't shout at him to shut up, although he still wanted to. "What does that even mean?"

"I don't *know*," Aaron said, and there was more animation in his voice than Call had expected. "I'm not — it takes a lot of concentration to pay attention to what's going on. Sometimes I feel like I'm slipping away. And sometimes I feel like I could do bad things and not really feel anything about them. So, you see, I really can't be the person who tells you right from wrong, Call. I really, really can't."

Call wanted to protest like he had before, but this time he stopped himself. He thought of the flat look in Aaron's eyes, the way he hadn't understood why he was supposed to care if the people in the Magisterium died. He couldn't keep insisting Aaron was fine. If Aaron believed something was wrong, then he owed it to Aaron to believe him.

And at least Aaron could tell. That had to mean something. If he wasn't Aaron, he wouldn't have been bothered
about how different he felt.

"We can fix this," Call said instead.

"Death isn't the same as a flat tire," Aaron said.

"We have to stay positive," said Call. "We just need to —"

"Someone's coming." Aaron stood up and pointed back
toward the house. The front door was open and a line of mages,
headed by Master Joseph, was marching toward them.

Call stood up, too. With Tamara and Jasper gone,
Call's plans of escape had become vague and half-formed.
He'd been distracted by Aaron's return and he'd thought that
Master Joseph had been distracted, too. He'd figured he had
more time.

Aaron looked up. Call followed his gaze — the sky was
heavy with iron-gray clouds, and through them Call could see
huge shapes wheeling.

One of them broke through the clouds. It was a massive air
elemental, with clear, ragged wings. On its back was Anastasia,
her silver-and-white armor stained and dirty.

Her elemental landed in the field behind Call and Aaron,
sending a wave of air that flattened the grass all around her in
a circle. Call glanced about — they were effectively trapped
between Anastasia on one side and Master Joseph on the other.

What was going on?

"Callum!" Master Joseph reached them first. Call noticed
two things immediately: Alex wasn't with him, and his coat

was splashed with some questionable-looking fluid. "The time has come."

Call exchanged a look with Aaron. "Time for what?"

"Tamara and Jasper were able to reach the Magisterium," said Anastasia, approaching them. Her elemental waited in the field behind her, rippling a little in the breeze. "The Assembly will soon know our location and what you've done."

"It's time for us to reveal ourselves, to show the world the power we have," said Master Joseph. "Hugo, did you bring the machine?"

Call and Aaron both stared as Hugo handed Master Joseph an enormous glass jar. Inside it, gray and black air swirled.

Tornado phone, Call mouthed at Aaron, who nodded slowly.

With a flourish, Master Joseph ripped the lid from the jar. The air swirled up around them violently. Anastasia's air elemental made a startled sound and disappeared with a pop.

Call moved closer to Aaron, whose hair was whipping across his eyes. The air expanded outward, slashing through the branches of the trees, circling the space where they stood.

"Master Rufus!" Master Joseph shouted. "Assembled mages! Show yourselves!"

It was like looking at a fuzzy television set. Slowly their images evolved, and Call could see the Assembly room and the green-robed mages there. He recognized some of them, like Tamara's parents, and of course the mages of the Magisterium — Master Milagros and Master North, Master

Rockmaple, and, sitting with his shoulders hunched, his bald head gleaming, Master Rufus.

They must have come together like this for one reason: to discuss how to defeat Callum Hunt, the Enemy of Death.

Call felt his stomach tighten at the sight of his teacher. But it was nothing compared to the feeling inside him a moment later when he saw who sat next to Rufus — Jasper, in the white uniform of Fourth Year, and Tamara, also in white, her hair in neat braids. Her wide, dark eyes seemed to stare out of the spell's vision, as if she were looking right into Call's soul.

It was Tamara's father who stepped forward, hand on her shoulder. "This is the last time we will offer you surrender, Master Joseph. The last war cost us all, but it cost you, too. You lost your sons, you lost Constantine, and you lost your way. If we go to battle again, there will be no brokering of peace. We will kill you and every Chaos-ridden thing we can find."

Call shuddered, thinking of Havoc, who was probably hiding behind a tree.

"Don't be ridiculous," Master Joseph said. "You try to argue as though you are in a position of strength, when we have the key to eternity. Is it because Tamara and Jasper ran back to you with news of our stronghold? If I was afraid of that getting out, I would have cut their throats when I had the chance."

Tamara glared at him, while Jasper took a step back. His mother was beside him, but Call couldn't spot his father anywhere.

"You don't understand," Master Joseph went on. "No one cares about your ridiculous war. Mages want their loved ones back. They want to live forever. The only way you could get the mage world on your side is to deny what is standing right beside me." With that, he put an arm around Aaron, who stepped out of his embrace.

"Say something," Master Joseph told Aaron.

"I have nothing to say," Aaron said to the mages. "I'm not on your side."

Call expected Master Joseph to yell at Aaron or try to stop him from speaking. But instead a wide smile spread over his face.

A hush went over the mages. Master Rufus raised his head from his hands. His face looked older, more lined. *"Aaron? Is that really you?"*

"I — I don't know," Aaron said.

But the Assembly was already in pandemonium. Whatever Tamara and Jasper had told them, Call thought, they hadn't really believed that Aaron had been brought back. They must have thought Aaron was Chaos-ridden, that Master Joseph was delusional. That Call was —

What had they thought Call was?

Master Rufus was looking at him now. His dark eyes were resigned. Disappointed. "Callum," he said. *"You* did this? You raised Aaron from the dead?"

Call looked down at his feet. He couldn't stand to meet Master Rufus's eyes.

"Of course he did," said Master Joseph. "The soul is the soul. Its essence doesn't change. He's always been Constantine Madden and he always will be."

"That's not true!"

Call looked up, startled, to see who had defended him. It was Tamara. She had her fists clenched at her sides. She wasn't looking at him, but she *had* said it. Did that mean she didn't believe what she'd said before, that he really was the Enemy?

Tamara's parents shushed her, pulling her to the side and almost out of Call's view, just as Master Joseph snorted in contempt.

"You are being very foolish," he said. "You think that if you attack us, we will be a small force — as Tamara and Jasper have no doubt reported. But do you really think I have no allies among you? All over the mage world are those who have been waiting for the news that we have completed Constantine's project. That we have conquered death. Already the messages have gone out. You may have noticed you are missing a few members . . ."

Several Assembly members glanced around, a few toward Jasper and his mother, at the space that Jasper's father should have occupied.

"You can't win," said Master Joseph. "Too many believe what we believe. What use is being born with magic if we are forbidden from profiting from it, if instead we must use it to control elementals for the good of a world that doesn't care about us? What is the good of magic if we cannot use it to solve the largest mystery in existence — the one that science has never penetrated — the mystery of the soul. Mages from all over the world will flock to our side now that we know the dead can live again."

A few of the mages began whispering in the back of the room, pointing. Call could tell that Aaron's presence, despite Aaron's disavowing of Master Joseph, had rattled them. Call wondered how many of them might flock to Master Joseph's side.

"Callum, Alastair has been frantic," Master Rufus said. "Meet with us. Bring Aaron. Let us at least verify these claims."

"You must think we are fools!" Master Joseph shouted at the shimmering images of the mages.

"We told you," Tamara said. "He's being held prisoner."

"It doesn't look like that to me," Assemblyman Graves said with a sniff. "And since you were involved in breaking him out of jail, we know you've been compromised."

"Call might have a little Stockholm syndrome," Jasper admitted. "But Master Joseph is keeping him there. He's keeping Aaron there, too."

"Are you holding those children captive?" Master Rufus demanded.

Master Joseph smiled. "Keeping Constantine Madden prisoner? I have always been his servant, nothing more. Call, are you being held here against your will?"

Call considered what to say next. A part of him wanted to scream for help, to plead for someone to save him. But it wasn't like the Assembly was going to be able to get him out — not right now. Better that Master Joseph believed he was on his side. If there was going to be a war, it was Call's job to do whatever he could to help the Assembly win.

At least, he *thought* he was supposed to help the Assembly win.

Either way, his answer was the same.

"No," he said, drawing himself up. "I am not a prisoner. I am Callum Hunt, the Enemy of Death reborn. And I accept my destiny."

↑ ≈ △ ○ @

"I don't like it here," Aaron said.

They were in Tamara's room, or what had been Tamara's room, sitting on the pink fluffy bed. Call's room still had holes punched into the walls, which made it pretty chilly, and house repairs were not at the top of anyone's to-do list.

"We won't be here for long," Call promised, although he only had the vaguest of plans.

Aaron shrugged. "I guess we're not going back to the Magisterium. Not after you announced you were the Enemy of Death."

Call wrapped his arms around his knees. "Did you think I meant it?"

"Did you mean it?" Aaron's eyes were expressionless. Call wondered what he thought. He used to be able to guess pretty well what Aaron was thinking, but not anymore. "You conquered death, after all."

"Tonight we go figure out what we can do about you," Call said. "After that, we run." He didn't mention the Chaos-ridden army, which Call hoped to bring along with them. If he could figure out what was going on with Aaron tonight, then they could go. They could march across the river before dawn and there was no way Alex had enough Chaos-ridden of his own to stop them.

But what if he couldn't? Should they go anyway? Did he really think that the mage world would accept him, especially now, with Aaron?

He remembered the faces of the Assembly and a cold pit formed in his stomach.

He thought of Anastasia's words: *You are powerful. You can't just give up that power. The world won't let you. It won't allow you to simply hide and be safe. It may come to this — ruling the world or being crushed under its boot heel.*

He really hoped she wasn't right about that, but he had to admit, she'd been right about Tamara.

"It's not going to be easy to get to the experiment room," said Aaron. "There are so many people around. It's chaos down there." It was true; the whole house was in an uproar, Anastasia rushing back and forth with the younger mages to summon elementals, Master Joseph out with Hugo and a few others, scrawling defense symbols in the land around the house.

Call wanted to say something clever, like chaos was his middle name, but it was too sad. He might still be a chaos mage, but Aaron wasn't — his magic belonged to Alex now. "Havoc's going to help," he said.

Havoc, on hearing his name, perked up his ears. He raced downstairs beside them, pausing at the bottom of the steps to look around with narrowed eyes and a low growl. Havoc had never much liked it here and seemed to like it less the longer they remained.

"Here's what you have to do." Call leaned down to tell the Chaos-ridden wolf.

↑ ≈ △ ○ ◎

As Call and Aaron descended the stairs, Call could hear the plan working. Havoc was barking and running around, leading the mages on a merry chase. They were all trying to figure out what set him off, sure it meant the Assembly was attacking.

As Havoc scampered around, Call and Aaron went straight to the experiment room, closing the door and locking it behind them.

It was only then they realized they weren't alone. Alex was sitting on the floor, an array of books open around him in a strange circle. He was sunken-eyed and his skin looked blotchy.

On a gurney on the other end of the room was a bizarre dead body. The corpse was that of a grown person, but with a face that appeared a grotesque parody of Drew's more childlike features. It looked as though it had been sculpted out of flesh, but with a butter knife. It was dressed in a parody of kid clothes: a shirt with a horse on it and red jeans. Just looking at it made Call's stomach churn.

"Uh," he said. "Sorry. We didn't know anyone else was in here."

Aaron just looked at Alex silently. There might even have been a small smile playing around the corners of his mouth.

Alex pushed himself to his feet, taking a few of the books with him. He pointed a shaking finger at Call. "*You!* You didn't explain what you did right. You lied." He tried to shoulder past where Call and Aaron were standing.

"Oh no," Call stopped him with a hand on his chest. Alex was taller than they were, but it was two to one, and Aaron was a lot more intimidating now that he was back from the dead. "You're going to help us."

"I'm not doing anything until you explain how you brought Aaron back — the truth, not what you've been saying to make Master Joseph torment me."

"I *did* tell you the truth. You just can't do it."

Alex looked straight at Call. For the first time the smirk was gone from his face. He looked sincerely scared. "Why? Why wouldn't I be able to do it? Why can't I just reach out and *find* his soul?"

Call shook his head. "I don't know. I didn't do that. We had Aaron's body. You don't *have* Drew's. How are you supposed to find his soul?"

The despair on Alex's face was obvious, but Master Joseph wasn't going to stop wanting his son to come back. Even if it was impossible, he was going to insist on it.

"So there's no hope," Alex said.

"I don't know," said Call. "You help me with Aaron and I'll help you with your problem."

Alex had been studying longer than he had — he'd been going after those Evil Overlord Points that Call had been fighting against for years. And if there was any chance that Alex had the key to helping Aaron, then it was worth taking.

Alex looked at Aaron and frowned. Aaron sat down on the floor, where Alex had been, and picked up a book.

"He seems fine," Alex grumbled. "Help you with what?"

"He's not happy," Call tried to explain.

Alex snorted. "Yeah, well, join the club. I'm not happy either. If I don't bring back Drew, I'm in deep trouble. Master Joseph keeps eyeing the Alkahest."

"Maybe you shouldn't have suggested he use it on me," Call said unsympathetically.

Alex sighed, not really having a retort for that. "So we're supposed to find some magical way to make Aaron happy again?"

Call frowned at Aaron, sitting on the floor, flipping pages as though he wasn't really paying attention to the conversation. "He's not unhappy, exactly," he said. "He's just — not in the right place. He's like a guy who took a train to a station and then had to get off and back on because he forgot his suitcase and now he's going the wrong way."

"Oh yeah," Alex said sarcastically. "That's much clearer."

Call didn't want to tell Alex everything Aaron had said — that seemed private. But he tried one more time. "Aaron doesn't have any magic. Fine, you stole his Makar abilities, but he should still be a mage, right? And he's not. Whatever is cutting him off from magic, that could be the missing part of him that's keeping him from feeling whole."

Alex hesitated.

"Besides," Call added, "if you brought back Drew without magic, that wouldn't exactly thrill Master Joseph."

Alex glared at him out of swollen eyes. "That's true," he said grudgingly. "All right, what are you suggesting?"

"We learned how to do the soul tap at the Magisterium," said Call. "I feel like I should try to look at Aaron's soul. Maybe see if I can tell what the problem is."

"What am I supposed to be here for?" Alex wanted to know.

Call took a deep breath. "You're older than us and you've been studying this longer. So think about what else we can check."

"And if we can't find anything wrong?"

"I could give him more of my soul," Call said in a low voice. "Maybe I just didn't give him enough."

Alex shook his head. "Your funeral," he said finally. "Aaron, get up on the experiment table."

Aaron looked over at the gurney with the corpse on it for a long moment. "No," he said. "I won't."

"It's occupied, anyway," Call said.

"We can dump the body on the floor," said Alex while Aaron eyed him with distaste.

To prevent that, Call dragged a book-covered table from a corner to the center of the room. They cleared off the surface and Aaron climbed up on it and lay down, his hands crossed over his chest.

Call took a deep breath, feeling self-conscious, trying to remember how it had been to see Aaron's soul before. This was the part he had to do alone. Alex didn't deserve to see anyone's soul, and definitely not Aaron's.

Call closed his eyes, took a deep breath, and began. It was harder than it had been back in the Magisterium. Aaron's resurrected body seemed to repel Call from being able to see through to the soul. It was surrounded by a kind of murkiness. He tried to hold on to memories of Aaron — Aaron laughing, and uncomplainingly eating lichen in the Refectory, and sorting sand, and dancing with Tamara. But they came dimly. What stuck out most clearly was Aaron's body, still and cold on the gurney in this room.

He pushed himself to remember what it had been like to put a piece of his soul into Aaron — like electricity lighting up metal in the darkness. The memory washed over him and he finally felt a path open to Aaron's presence. He saw the light of a soul, pale and clear, with a kind of golden light that was all Aaron.

But dark tendrils surrounded it, hooking it in place, worming into it the way roots of ivy worm their way into buildings until the stonework crumbles. His body seemed to pulse with chaos energy. Call reached out with his mind and felt a terrible overwhelming coldness.

The body. There was something wrong with Aaron's body.

"What are you doing?" The doors of the experiment room burst open. Dazed, Call leaned against the table as Alex yelped and jumped backward.

It was Master Joseph, and he looked furious.

CHAPTER THIRTEEN

CALL TOOK A step back from Aaron, stumbling over a stray book. This was Master Joseph as Call hadn't seen him before — wild-eyed and full of rage. He wore the Alkahest over one hand.

At the sight of it, Call's breath caught.

Always before, even in the depths of his anger, Master Joseph had protected Call. In the tomb of the Enemy of Death, he'd even thrown himself in front of Call, ready to toss his own life away to save him. But now, he looked ready to murder Call without thinking twice.

"H-helping Aaron," Call stammered.

"You cannot meddle with what you have done!" Master Joseph shouted, spit flying from his lips. "Without a resurrection, we are nothing! The mages will overrun us and we will be destroyed. It is only with the power of eternal life that our army can swell to destroy the Assembly!"

On the table, Aaron sat up. He didn't look intimidated by all the yelling. He just stared at Master Joseph impassively.

"Okay, okay," Call said, holding up his hands, placating. Alex had backed far enough away from Master Joseph that he was standing against the wall, his face the color of candlewax. Call had never seen Alex like that before and it made him even more scared. "Don't freak out. Everything's fine."

Master Joseph took a step toward Aaron and grabbed his neck, tilting his face and looking him over like an angry car owner trying to determine if his new Mercedes had a scratch on it.

"Callum seems to be determined to show me that he's more trouble than he's worth. From the beginning, he defied me. He mocked his role. He made light of the great honor bestowed on him. He threw my loyalty and my sacrifices back in my face, over and over again. Well, Callum, I think I've had enough of you ruining my plans."

"Don't take it personally," Call said. "Lots of people find me really annoying. It's not just you."

"Call was trying to help me," Aaron said, jerking back from Master Joseph's grip. There was something almost terrifying in his expression.

"You don't need help!" Master Joseph snapped, seizing him by the shoulder this time. "You shouldn't be tampered with!"

"Get off me," Aaron said, shoving Master Joseph's hand away. "You don't know what I need!"

Master Joseph snarled. "Be silent. You're not a person. You're a *thing*. A dead thing."

Aaron's arm shot out and he seized Master Joseph by the throat. It all happened fast — too fast for Call to react in any way but sucking in a sharp breath.

Master Joseph's hand came up, as though he were going to conjure up fire, but Aaron caught his arm and *twisted* it behind his back. His other hand tightened on Master Joseph's throat. Master Joseph thrashed, gasping for air, his gaze going unfocused.

"Don't!" Call shouted, finally realizing what Aaron meant to do. "Aaron, no!"

But Call had commanded Aaron never to obey him, and Aaron didn't. His fingers dug deeper into Master Joseph's throat and there was a popping, snapping sound, like the sound twigs made when you stepped on them.

The light went out of Master Joseph's eyes.

Call gasped, staring at Aaron, unwilling to believe that his friend had done this, his closest friend, who'd always also been the best person he knew. For the first time, Call was afraid — not *for* Aaron, but *of* him.

Alex was making a weird noise that turned out to be the word *no* said again and again, over and over.

Aaron let go of Master Joseph and stepped back, looking

at his hand as though he was only just then realizing what he had done. He seemed confused when Master Joseph's body hit the ground.

You're a thing. A dead thing.

Master Joseph lay slumped at Call's feet, like Drew before him. *Knowing me has been pretty bad for Master Joseph's family,* Call thought a little hysterically, but no part of that was actually funny.

Alex dropped to his knees. He was staring at Master Joseph's body. "You — you can bring him back," Alex said.

"But I won't." The words were out of Call's mouth before he even considered them. He was more than a little shocked that Alex had asked — the Master had threatened Alex with the Alkahest, had mocked and disparaged him. But Alex was staring at his body with a haunted look.

"You have to," Alex said. "Someone has to lead us."

Aaron stared blankly at what he'd done. If he felt remorse, he didn't show it.

Alex crept closer to Master Joseph's body. There were tears on his face, but he didn't reach to touch the dead mage. Instead his hand went to the Alkahest. He cradled it to his chest and Call realized that he'd been a fool to not grab for that before anything else.

"Uh, Alex?" Call said. "What are you doing?

"I never thought he could die," Alex didn't sound like he was talking to Call. His voice was low, like he was talking to himself. "He was a great man. I thought he would lead the army with me at his side."

"He was an evil man," Call said. "In a way, everything that happened — the mage war and Jericho's death and even Drew's death — was his fault. He hurt people."

"He is the only reason you were ever important at all. He believed in you. And you're just going leave him there?"

"Like you did with me?" Aaron said, sliding down off the table. He moved to stand next to Call.

"I didn't do that to show I was better than the Enemy of Death," Alex snarled. He still held the Alkahest, hugging it to himself.

"No," Call said. "You did it to show you were exactly like him." He walked to the door, Aaron behind him. There, Call turned back. "We're going to go. Look, I know you're upset, but you could do good out in the world with your chaos magic. You can still be famous and powerful and *not* on the side of evil. With Master Joseph gone, this can all be over."

Alex looked at him tiredly. "Good, evil," he said. "What's the difference?"

Call expected Aaron to say something. He expected him to point out that Alex must know the difference — but he didn't. Maybe this Aaron couldn't tell, either.

Call and Aaron walked down the corridor in silence and were quickly joined by Havoc, his ears back but his tail wagging. Footsteps sounded in the house, but no one stood between them and the door. They stepped out onto the lawn.

"Where are we going?" Aaron asked.

"I don't know," Call said. "Off this island. Away from everything."

"Am I coming with you?" Aaron seemed to have realized that killing Master Joseph was something that might matter to Call. Maybe some part of Aaron was bothered by it, too. Maybe he remembered that there was a time when he would never have killed someone like that, in cold blood, with his bare hands.

"Of course you are," Call said, but Aaron probably heard the hesitation in his voice.

"Good," Aaron said.

They started to walk toward the woods, following the road, sticking to the edge of the tree line. Call's leg started aching pretty quickly, but he didn't slow down. He let the pain happen, let it get worse. So what if it hurt? So what if he limped? The pain made him feel everything in sharper relief.

Aaron walked alongside him, seemingly lost in his own thoughts. Horrifyingly, the more time passed, the less Call felt like his friend was accompanying him and the more he felt as though it was one of the Chaos-ridden. Even Havoc seemed to be avoiding Aaron, sticking to the opposite side of Call, never darting over to be patted. Even though Havoc had nosed up to Aaron to be petted yesterday, it seemed clear the wolf thought Aaron had changed since he'd first returned to the living. Aaron *had* changed. But why would that have happened?

At least they were close to the water now. Call could hear the waves lapping at the bank. And then, suddenly, that noise was subsumed by the growl of engines. Trucks roared down the road. Overhead, a ribbonlike elemental cut through the sky.

Call turned, grabbed Aaron by the shoulder, and shoved him into the woods. "Run! We've got to run!" he said, though he knew his leg wasn't going to let him go fast.

And then, coming out of the woods was Hugo, more mages with him, and marching behind them, Alex's Chaos-ridden.

Even with Master Joseph dead, Call and Aaron weren't going to be allowed to leave.

"I am the Enemy of Death!" Call shouted. "I am the person in charge. It's my commands you're supposed to be listening to — and I say go back to the house! This is over. I am Constantine Madden! I am the Enemy of Death! And I say this is over!"

Hugo took a step toward Call, a smile on his face. With growing fear, Call realized that there weren't just the mages Call had seen before. Not just escapees from the Panopticon and trainees like Jeffrey. There were others — even people wearing Assembly robes, who must have just arrived. Traitors, all come to fight on the wrong side. Call even thought he recognized Jasper's dad.

Havoc started to bark loudly.

"You may have Constantine's soul but you're not in charge,"

Hugo said. "Master Joseph gave very specific instructions. If something were to happen to him, we're supposed to follow Alex Strike, and Alex says to bring you back — by force if necessary."

"But I'm the Enemy of Death!" Call said. "Look, I'm the one that resurrected Aaron. You're all here to unlock death's mysteries, right? Well I am the combination to death's locker! I am the key to the weird shed in its backyard!"

For a moment, after Call spoke, everyone was silent. He wasn't sure if he'd dazzled them with his logic or not. For a moment, he hoped they might really let him go.

"Maybe you're . . . all those things," Hugo said. "But you're still going to have to come back to the main house. There's going to be a battle soon, and we all need to be ready. It's not safe for you or for Aaron in the woods right now. Scouts from the Assembly could be anywhere."

"I'm not going back with you." Call raised his hand, calling on chaos. Maybe if he showed them what he was and what he could do, they'd let him go. Maybe if they realized he was going to fight, they would be afraid to hurt him. Power began to gather within him slowly. He had almost drained himself completely trying to see what was wrong with Aaron. With a piece of his soul missing, he was so weak. He needed more power.

Out of habit, he reached for Aaron, his counterweight. But reaching for him was like plunging an arm into icy water. A cold, black nothingness washed over his mind. Call gave a cry as the world went dark.

Call woke with his hands tied behind him, his head lolling to one side. For a moment after he regained consciousness, he thought he was back in the Panopticon. It was only when he saw his surroundings — Master Joseph's creepy Victorian parlor — that he remembered everything that had happened. Master Joseph . . . Tamara . . . Aaron.

Aaron.

Looking down, he saw that he was lashed to a chair, his ankles bound tightly to its legs and his wrists tied behind his back

"You're awake," Aaron said from behind him, close enough that Call was pretty sure he was lashed to a chair, too — probably the chairs were tied together. Call shuffled a little to test his assumption and the weight confirmed it.

"What happened?" Call asked.

Aaron shifted his weight a little. "You looked like you were going to do some magic and then you just passed out. I have no magic, so I couldn't do much. Neither could Havoc. They tied us up. Alex ran around a lot, giving orders. I think Hugo was telling the truth about a battle."

"Alex is really in charge?" Call said, incredulous.

"He's claiming —" Aaron started, but before he could finish, Hugo came into the room, Alex behind him. When the door opened, Call heard Anastasia talking to some other mages. For a moment, he thought he even heard a voice he recognized, but he couldn't place it.

Alex was clad in a long black coat buttoned to the neck, his hair carefully combed back from his face. He no longer looked tired or frightened. His eyes glittered, and he wore the Alkahest on one arm, gleaming as if it had just been polished.

"Seriously? You look like you're auditioning for the next Matrix movie," Call said, and then realized that maybe he shouldn't be so sassy while he was tied to a chair.

"I am in charge now, as I always should have been," Alex said. "I have all of Constantine's knowledge and all of Master Joseph's expertise. I am the new Enemy of Death."

Call had to bite his lip to prevent himself from making another joke.

"I could transfer your Makar power to myself and be the most powerful chaos user who ever lived. Either obey me and become my loyal lieutenant, Callum, or I will kill you right here."

"That's a compelling offer," Call said. "But are you even sure the Alkahest works like that?"

"You can't kill him," Aaron said softly. "Just like you can't kill me. Without us, your army won't stay."

Alex's mouth twisted into a sneer. "Of course they will."

"Of course they won't," said Call, running with Aaron's lead. "They care about the dead being brought back. I did that. You didn't. And everyone knows it."

"He's right," said Aaron. "They came to follow Call and Master Joseph, not some teenager they don't know."

Alex sneered. "Please. Call explained how to bring back the dead. He used his own soul. I can do the same thing any time I want, so I don't need him anymore. I need *you*, sure. *You're* the proof this works, but he's disposable."

"If he dies, I won't help you," Aaron said emotionlessly. "I might not help you anyway."

Alex looked ready to stamp his foot, but he drew a knife from the inside pocket of his coat instead. It was a nasty curved thing and it made Call think of Miri, his own blade, back at the Magisterium. He forced a grin. "Well, Call. Do you want to take the chance I will do it anyway or do you want to promise you'll be loyal? Will you fight on our side in the coming conflict?"

"I'll fight on your side," Call said. "After all, Aaron and I don't have anywhere else to go. Did you see me running after Tamara and Jasper? Didn't you hear me when I told the whole Assembly that I wasn't being held against my will? Everyone else hates me. You should have led with that."

Alex grinned and reached down to slash the knife through the ropes that held them. Call got to his feet, his bad leg aching. Aaron rose slowly after him.

"Come," Alex said, and marched from the room.

The sun had set while Call and Aaron had been tied up. It was dark outside the windows as they hurried along the hallway of the house behind Alex. As they passed through the parlor, Call could see that the huge lawns outside the house were lit with burning spheres of mage fire.

They reached the porch of the house and stood there, staring, Alex smirking beside them. In the flickering firelight, the lawn was an eerie battleground. A mass of mages in green Assembly robes and the black uniforms of the Magisterium faced the house. Standing with their backs to the house were Master Joseph's forces.

They were Alex's forces now. Call could mostly only see their backs, but there were a lot of them. He thought he recognized Hugo and some of the other mages. They formed a wall several lines deep in front of the house, staring ahead with grim determination.

There was a gap of about a football field's length between them and the mages of the Assembly. Call moved toward the porch railing, and heard a bark.

"Havoc!" he said. The wolf bounded around the side of the house and up the steps to press himself against Call's leg. Call winced in pain but reached down to ruffle Havoc's fur. It was a relief to see Havoc, the only one of his friends who hadn't changed.

He chanced a sideways look at Aaron. Aaron's profile was sharp in the red-orange light. It made his green eyes look blacker. He thought of the way Aaron had squeezed Master Joseph's throat until it snapped, and he felt an ache inside. In a way he missed Aaron more now than he had when Aaron was dead. It was as if he'd brought Aaron back and since that moment, everything that had made Aaron himself had been evaporating from him, like mist off a river.

But why? The thought teased the edge of Call's mind. It was Aaron's body that was the problem. If he had put him in a different body — if he had moved Aaron's soul, the way Constantine had moved his own — would it have made any difference?

Havoc barked again as the front door opened and Anastasia came out onto the porch. She wore her silver-and-white armor, now clean, her hair up in a massive pewter twist. She glided toward Call.

"Callum," she said. "I'm glad you've seen sense and decided to fight alongside Alex."

"I didn't see sense," Call said. "He just threatened to kill me otherwise."

She blinked. Call couldn't help but wonder: Didn't it matter to her, the idea that Alex might kill Constantine's soul? But whatever compromises Anastasia had made long ago in order to accept what her son had done and want him back anyway seemed to be fogging her mind.

"Once the battle is over," she said, "we'll go somewhere, and we'll raise Jericho, and we'll live in peace."

"That's enough, Anastasia," said Alex. "Master Joseph tolerated this ridiculous delusion, but I won't. Callum isn't your son. I don't care what you think. He isn't Constantine Madden, and all your fawning over him won't make any difference. He doesn't love you."

There was an immediate sharpening in Anastasia's expression. The fog was lifting and Call wasn't sure that Alex was going to like whatever was underneath.

"Alex, you would do well to remember that you need me," Anastasia said. "And my elementals."

"And *you'd* do well to remember that if you should consider anyone your son, it's me."

"I know Call's soul," said Anastasia, though Call didn't think that was true. "Not yours."

Alex's face twisted.

"There are a lot of things here," Aaron interrupted, as if no one had been speaking. Alex glared; Call looked around the island.

It was true. The army of the Chaos-ridden had been marched out of the lake. They stood in neat rows, their clothing in tatters from such a long submersion in the water. Near them were elementals: long, airy snakes coiling among the trees, flaming lizards, enormous spiders made entirely from rock. Call didn't see any water elementals, but if there were any, they were probably frolicking in the river.

Call looked again at the mages. He'd thought he heard a familiar voice before, but now he realized he knew *several* of the people there. A few Assembly members stood near Hugo, along with several parents he recognized from the Magisterium. Jasper's father was there, causing Call to suck in a breath.

But moving through the crowd toward Alex was someone who gave Call a bigger shock — Tamara's older sister Kimiya.

A moment later, she had thrown herself into Alex's arms. "I'm so glad you're all right," she said breathlessly.

Even Alex looked surprised. "Kimiya?"

"Kimiya, what are you thinking?" Call demanded. "You should be on the same side as your sisters."

Kimiya turned to look at him angrily. "Ravan isn't my sister," she said. "She was destroyed by fire. Now she's a monster. My best friend, Jen, is dead —" Her lips trembled. "I hate death," she said. "If Alex wants to destroy death, then I want to be at his side."

Alex shot Call a superior look over Kimiya's head. "Go and get yourself a weapon, darling," he said, stroking her long black hair. "We'll fight together."

Kimiya disappeared inside. Alex grinned at Call, who barely restrained himself from lunging at Alex and strangling him. Alex cut him off, though, by moving up beside him and grabbing him by the back of the shirt with the hand that wasn't enveloped by the Alkahest. Hugo, beside him, seized Aaron.

"Loyal followers!" Alex shouted, and Call and Aaron were shoved forward and down the steps, into the center of a bright spotlight that was being cast by several mages. "Here they are! Callum Hunt, the reincarnation of Constantine Madden, and his greatest accomplishment — Aaron Stewart, raised from the dead!"

A cheer went up. Call heard people shouting Aaron's name. He felt dizzy. It was so much like the time Aaron had been declared the Makar, the hero of the Magisterium, and yet it was nothing like that.

"And now —" Alex began. But Hugo interrupted him.

"Master Strike," he said. "Look. The other side is waving a flag of parlay."

"They surrender?" Alex sounded disappointed. "Already?"

Hugo shook his head. "It means they want to talk before the battle."

"They sent us a message. They do want to talk." Anastasia strode up, her expression taut. "But only to Call."

"No," Alex said. "I forbid it."

Aaron looked ready to argue on his behalf, but Call put a hand on his arm.

"Good," he said to Alex. "They'd probably grab me, figuring that the army would be useless without me."

"*I* am leading this army," Alex said fiercely.

Call smirked. "I'm still the Enemy of Death."

Alex turned to Anastasia. He looked petulant enough to stamp a foot. "Why do they want to talk to Callum?"

Kimiya had reappeared from the house, holding an axe made of stone. It bore numerous air and earth symbols carved into it, which Call suspected made it light enough to hold. "It was Tamara's idea," she said. "Tamara persuaded our parents he could be trusted. That his word would be good." She shook her head. "Really, I think she wants to say good-bye one more time."

A cruel smirk grew on Alex's face. "I didn't know you and Tamara had something going on, Callum."

"It's not like that." The whine in Call's voice sounded

ridiculous, ridiculous enough that Aaron raised his eyebrows. He could tell that Call was faking.

"I was wrong. You *are* going, Callum Hunt," Alex said with a laugh, clearly believing he was upsetting Call. "You're going to go and say exactly what I want you to say. You will bring my words to the mages of the Assembly and they will learn who the real leader of this army is."

Call tried to look sullen, but his guts were churning. Here was his chance to help the Assembly. But help them how?

He took a deep breath. He needed to give them an idea of the forces they were going to be up against. A rough head count of elementals and Chaos-ridden and mages. They were going to want that. And they'd want to know that Master Joseph was dead.

"Don't come back," Aaron whispered to him.

Call shook his head. "And leave you here? No."

Aaron said nothing more. He didn't insist, didn't explain.

"I heard that," Alex said. He looked like a dark bird of prey, wrapped in black, glaring with hooded eyes at the mages of the Assembly. "I will be watching to see if you run to them, Call. If you try to turn traitor. And if you do, then I will command every one of the Chaos-ridden to attack and not stop until they kill you."

Kimiya gave a little gasp. Call turned to see that a fiery line was spreading from the line of the Assembly mages across the empty grass, toward Alex's forces.

The grass didn't burn — the fire seemed to sail over it, expanding as it flew. Alex narrowed his eyes. "They're coming for us," he said. "Call, help me order the Chaos-ridden —"

"No." Kimiya put her hand on Alex's wrist. "It's Ravan."

"She's *attacking*!" Alex's voice rose to a screech, but Ravan had already reached them. She had become a column of blaze and fire, rising from the grass, gray smoke streaked with orange lines of flame.

The smoke coalesced. It became more and more solid, until a gray girl stood in front of them. She was solid and real-seeming. The folds of a gray smoke dress blew around her. Her hair was long, and had once been black. Now it gleamed dusty silver. Her face reminded Call of Tamara, and he felt a twisting deep inside.

Three of the mages sent up an icy shield between her and Alex's forces but she only laughed.

"I will escort Callum Hunt to the site of parlay," she said. "I am peaceable now, but if you strike me I will burn the earth for a mile around."

Could she really do that? Call wondered. How bad was this magical battle going to get?

"Monster," said Kimiya in a revolted voice.

Ravan gave a little, tilted smile. "Sister," she said to Kimiya, and reached out a hand to gesture Call to walk in front of her. "Callum. We must hurry."

Call gave Aaron a look that said that he would come back,

before he walked around the ice shield and followed Tamara's sister across the grass.

Everything was eerily quiet. There was hardly even any wind as they moved across the grass, allowing Ravan to keep her human shape. As they grew closer to the other side, Call saw that three figures were waiting for him. Master Rufus's dark skin stood out in contrast to his dark olive Assembly robes. Beside him was Tamara, in her school uniform, her hair very black against the white. And next to Tamara was Jasper. His face was blank and angry as he watched Call approach.

As Call reached them, Ravan began to scatter. Ash flowed away from her in waves. For a moment, as she dissolved, she looked at Call. Her eyes were orange, full of flames.

"*Don't hurt my sister,*" she whispered. "*She cares for you.*"

And then she was gone.

Call came to a stop in front of them — his friend, his once-girlfriend, and his former teacher. None of them spoke.

"Call —" Tamara started.

"I don't have a lot of time," Call interrupted her. He didn't think he could bear to hear what she had to say. He started talking fast, not looking at any of them directly. He began to outline what Alex's army consisted of and what had happened to Master Joseph. As he spoke, one of the Assembly members — Graves — broke free of the others and strode over to them. He'd never been a big fan of Call's, and Call tried to ignore that he was there.

As Call wound down, Master Rufus's expression changed from neutral to concerned.

"Callum," he interrupted, finally. "You're telling me that Master Joseph is *dead*? And that Alex Strike and Anastasia Tarquin are leading the troops?"

Call nodded. "Mostly Alex, though. Look, I surrender! I surrender! This was all a huge mistake. Just promise that nothing is going to happen to Aaron and I'll do whatever you want."

At his name, all of their expressions darkened. Graves pointed a skinny finger at him. "Callum Hunt, what you have done may have created a rift in the mage world that can never heal. The dead are not meant to return. Aaron must be destroyed, for the sake of his soul, if for no other reason."

"Is that what you think?" Call turned to Tamara.

Her eyes were shimmering as if she was holding back tears, but her voice was firm. "I think you brought back part of Aaron but not all of him," Tamara told him. "I don't think he would want to live like this."

But what if I'm starting to understand what I did wrong? he wanted to ask her, but he already knew the answer. It was too late. *What if I can still fix it? Fix him?*

Call wasn't sure that was possible. It was just the germ of a thought in the back of his mind. Something about Aaron's body, a body that had been dead — his own body had been living when Constantine had pushed his soul into it —

But what he was thinking about might be something that could never be done.

Should never be done.

"Let it be Aaron's choice," Call said, looking at his shoes.

"As if he can make choices," Graves snorted. "Can he even talk?"

Tamara reddened. Call glared at Graves. "Yes, he can choose to do things. He's the one who killed Master Joseph, and he did it all on his own."

Tamara caught her breath. "Aaron killed Master Joseph?"

"Yes," Call said. "And he should be allowed to decide if he lives or dies and where he goes! I brought him back. I owe him that."

"It hardly matters," said Graves, though he looked shaken. "You cannot come back to the Magisterium."

"Then send me back to the Panopticon," said Call. "Put me in prison. Just not him."

"You can't come back to us, Callum," Rufus said gently, but Graves interrupted him:

"We didn't parlay with you to offer you and your monster help. We asked to speak with you because your family and friends believe you can be persuaded to do the right thing." He looked around as if he couldn't believe how stupid Call's friends were.

"The right thing?" Call echoed, not at all sure what they were suggesting. The only thing he was sure of was that he wasn't going to like it.

Graves went on. "We have gone to war against the forces of the Enemy before. And yes, perhaps Alex is much diminished, but his forces aren't. He is a Makar and there is no Makar fighting on our side anymore."

Call opened his mouth, but Jasper shook his head, and for once, Call shut it. He wished that his father had been allowed to come to this parlay. He imagined that Alastair must have argued for it, but he understood why they hadn't let him come. Alastair would cut to the chase and tell him what was really happening.

"We have had more traitors and defectors than we supposed. There's only one way to end this for good. You must use your chaos magic to destroy Alex Strike — and yourself."

Call sucked in a breath.

"*What?*" demanded Jasper.

Tamara exploded with anger. "That's not what we agreed to! It was that he should destroy Master Joseph and then everything would be forgiven!" She whirled around to face Call. "I told them you didn't mean it when you said you were the Enemy of Death, that you were just saying it so Alex and Master Joseph didn't know you were on our side. I know you brought Aaron back because you care about him, Call, and not for any other reason."

"Graves, this is insupportable," said Rufus. "He is a child. You cannot ask him to destroy himself."

"He is the Enemy of Death," said Graves. "He said so himself."

Call started to back away. He felt sick. Master Rufus might argue, but the Assembly had already decided, and the Assembly called the shots. They wanted him dead. There was nothing he could do about it.

"Call," Master Rufus said. "Call, come back —"

But Call was gone, sprinting across the grass toward Alex's army, toward Anastasia Tarquin and the Chaos-ridden. He'd spent so much time trying to escape them, he never thought he'd be fleeing toward them.

Havoc ran to greet him, barking, his coruscating eyes shining in the moonlight like points of fire. Call grabbed his ruff and ran the rest of the way, half leaning on the wolf, his bad leg aching along with his head.

He would have gone back to the house, but too many Chaos-ridden and Assembly traitors blocked his way. Alex stood beside Kimiya and Anastasia. He was grinning. Aaron was slightly behind him. Hugo had a hand on his shoulder — not a friendly hand, but a warning one.

"So how'd you like that, Call?" Alex said. "Kimiya told me they wanted you to sacrifice yourself to take out Master Joseph. She overheard Graves talking about it. Nice to know how much the Magisterium really values you, huh?"

Call felt his heart sink further. That was why Alex had let him go to the parlay. Not because he trusted Call or because he'd been deceived by his pretending to be upset, but because he believed Call wouldn't sacrifice himself.

And he'd been right. Call had run away from the Assembly mages. Call thought back to his first year learning magic. The end of his private Cinquain. *Call wants to live.*

"Tamara," Kimiya said. "Was Tamara all right? She's not going to fight, is she?"

Call opened his mouth, then shut it again. Kimiya didn't deserve to know about Tamara. Didn't deserve to pretend to care about Tamara when she'd abandoned her.

"I've got the Alkahest," said Alex, raising his arm. "You fight with us, Call, or you die and Aaron dies. Now you see that, right?"

Call took a deep breath, trying to steady himself. He felt like screaming. He felt like crying. But he couldn't do either one.

"Yeah, they made me an insulting offer. So what? They already abandoned me." Call looked Alex in the face, trying to turn his anger into confidence. "I already said I had nowhere else to go."

Alex's smile tilted. "Glad to hear they didn't change your mind."

Aaron came over to him but didn't ask how he was, didn't put an arm on his shoulder. "A lot of people are going to die today, aren't they?" he asked instead. He didn't sound particularly concerned, just curious.

"I guess so," Call said. It still seemed impossible, stupid, but it was happening. A lot of people — good people — were going to get hurt. They were going to die like his mother died.

"You're going to lead the Enemy of Death's Chaos-ridden on the left flank," Alex told him. "I am going to lead my own on the right. Anastasia is going to head up the elementals from above. Hugo will lead the mages, who will support us from a safe distance. We will crush them. You don't mind being on the front lines, right?"

"Of course not," Call said. He was sure Alex considered Constantine's Chaos-ridden the most expendable and was willing to sacrifice Call the first chance he got. Maybe even arrange a little accident.

"Aaron is going to stay with me," Alex said, making the "accident" scenario even more likely.

"I don't want to do that," said Aaron in an even tone that made Call a little nervous.

"Well, you're going to," Alex said. "But don't worry about Call. He won't be all alone. Havoc can go with him."

At the sound of his name, the Chaos-ridden wolf barked once.

Call looked over at Aaron. He would have insisted that his friend come with him — if it wasn't that Alex was going to put Call in the most danger possible and that meant Aaron would be in it, too.

He thought about what Graves had said to him as he called the Chaos-ridden to him and commanded them to arrange themselves in neat little rows. They looked like an army of toy soldiers, grown massive and terrifying.

Call had been trying to avoid this exact moment ever since he'd found out that his soul had once belonged to Constantine Madden. It had been his fear that he would become like the Enemy of Death, that he'd be the cause of pain and fear and death. He'd been trying to make good choices, but though each choice had seemed fine all by itself — well, *most* of the choices had seemed fine — they'd still led him here.

He could make excuses, but excuses didn't matter. Graves being such a jerk didn't matter, because he was right. Even if none of this was Call's fault, he was still the only one who could fix it.

He just had to figure out how.

"Move out," Alex said. "Order them."

"Okay," Call said to his Chaos-ridden. "Time to march."

"Yessss," they groaned, in the language that only Call understood. And they began to move.

Their feet thundered over the ground as they headed toward where the Assembly's army was still massing at the water's edge. The air above them crackled with elemental magic. Behind them came Alex's Chaos-ridden and the mages.

Call had never felt so unprepared for anything in his life. *It's just like the Iron Trial,* he told himself. *All you have to do is lose.*

He was going to make sure his side lost spectacularly.

CHAPTER FOURTEEN

IT WAS LIKE pictures Call had seen of the last Mage War, the one where Verity Torres had died on the field facing Constantine Madden.

Only now he *was* Verity, getting ready to die. Aaron had told Call about fearing he would die on the field like Verity had, a Makar sacrificed to the good of the Assembly of Mages. But it was Call who would die like that. Call, who the Assembly hated.

He was Verity and Constantine both, somehow. He thought about them as he marched ahead of the Chaos-ridden, Havoc at his side. He could hear their whispers in their strange dead language. They were asking him for instructions, asking what he wanted.

His flank was approaching the Assembly mages from the west. He could see Alex closing in from the east — Alex, wearing the silver mask of the Enemy of Death. He looked inhuman in it, half ghost and half monster. Call heard Alex shout and saw the Alkahest flash copper in the air as Alex gestured for his Chaos-ridden to attack.

They burst forward around him, and the Assembly traitors — all of whom had been put under Hugo's command — surged forward, too. Only Aaron didn't move. He stood where he was, a lone dark figure, the forgotten once-Makar, like a stone in the middle of a river as the Chaos-ridden streamed forward around him.

They slammed into the eastern flank of the Assembly mages and there was screaming. Call looked in horror for Tamara and Jasper, but he couldn't see any students among the fighters. He hoped they'd been pushed to the back of the lines, where they'd be protected.

There was no longer any cleared earth between the two lines of fighters. There was only pandemonium — Jasper's father exchanging bolts of sharpened ice with Master Rufus. Master Rockmaple fending off several Chaos-ridden with a curving alchemical sword. It sliced into their bodies and they collapsed and lay twitching.

Ravan hovered, wreathed in smoke, in the air above the Assembly mages, trading bursts of fire with Anastasia. Part of Anastasia's uniform was scorched black, but she was holding her own.

"Call!" It was Alex shouting, furiously, over the smash and crash of the battle. "Call, *attack!*"

Call took a deep breath. He knew what he had to do. With the Chaos-ridden under his command, Alex's side might be able to overwhelm the Assembly's mages. Without them, it would be much harder for Alex to win.

Call drew on the magic of the void to bind his will to the Chaos-ridden under his command so that they would understand his wishes fully. "You, who I have created!" he called. "*Dance!*"

Immediately, like a flash mob, they carried out the synchronized moves Call willed. They kicked up their legs and spun around, moaning in time to a melody no one else could hear. They threw their hands in the air. They boogied. They got *down*.

It was totally ridiculous. It was so ridiculous that for a moment, everyone else paused. Even the elementals seemed curious.

A few mages even laughed.

But Alex wasn't laughing. He looked absolutely furious.

"You *idiot!*" he shouted, flying toward where Call stood. "You've made a fool out of me for the last time!"

The silver mask caught the light and Call saw his own reflection in it. Then Alex pulled it off. Underneath, his face had gone red with rage. The Alkahest gleamed on his other arm and Call had no doubt what he was planning.

At least Call was sure his Chaos-ridden were occupied and would be for a while. He had willed enough magic into his commands that they would be hard for Alex to disrupt, but it had left Call depleted even before the fight started. And given how his magic drained faster since he'd given away part of his soul, beating Alex wasn't going to be easy.

Still, he didn't need to survive to win.

Using his power, Call ripped a hole into the void. He could feel the Chaos there, cold and oily and pulsing with the promise of enormous power.

Alex brought up the arm holding the Alkahest and pointed it straight at Call. Call tried to draw on chaos, to send it at Alex, but he was too slow.

Havoc got there first.

The Chaos-ridden wolf leaped at Alex, biting down on his metal-covered wrist. The beam that should have hit Call hit him instead.

"Havoc!" Call shouted. But the beam had smashed into Havoc's chest, lifting the wolf into the air. Havoc's body went limp and he hit the ground hard.

Call stopped thinking about magic, about wars, about anything. Pushing past the pain in his leg, he lurched toward Alex and punched him in the face.

The older boy staggered back. His lip was split and he looked more surprised than anything else. Call's knuckles hurt. He'd never hit anyone before.

With a sneer, Alex slammed the Alkahest into the side of Call's head, sending Call sprawling in the grass of the field.

He could see Havoc's body, sprawled in the field a little distance from him. The wolf wasn't moving.

Call stood as Alex aimed the Alkahest again. And then Aaron was there, wrenching it off his arm. The two of them struggled, hanging on to opposite ends of it.

"Chaos-ridden!" Alex shouted. "To me!"

Crawling to Havoc, Call covered his wolf's body with his own and called on chaos again. It spiraled around him, dark with promise.

He fed it with rage. Rage at Master Joseph for taking his choices away, for kidnapping him and forcing him to be Constantine. Rage at death, for taking away Aaron. For taking away his mother. For taking Havoc. For leaving him with a torn black gaping hole of loss in the middle of his heart.

He fed the chaos with rage and loss, with grief, and finally with fear, the fear of his own death, fear of what lay on the other side of his sacrifice.

As he fed the chaos, he felt the energy pour out of him. Everything inside him was going into spilling out the power of nothingness. Alex was screaming as the heavy black coils circled him like the coils of a snake.

Call gasped. He felt the gravity of the earth pulling him down. He was weakening. He could see Aaron standing alone on the battlefield. The Chaos-ridden ignored Aaron's presence: He was nothing to them, not a mage, and maybe, like them, not even really alive.

Aaron was staring at Call. He was shaking his head, and Call knew that it was because Call ought to be reaching for his counterweight right now. But Call didn't have a counterweight — and even if he had, he wasn't sure he would have reached out. This was too much magic. It licked at his soul.

Alex sent chaos back at him, a coiling choking cloud that drew him into it.

He thought of Ravan, of how she must have felt using so much fire magic that she became a Devoured of fire. He saw her now, flying through the air in a spray of sparks. No longer human. He didn't want to become a creature of chaos. And so, with the last of his magic, he pushed the chaos away — thrust it all back into the void and thrust Alex with it. Alex fought, sending spiraling arrows of nothingness at Call, but Call scraped the very bottom of his own soul for power.

Alex's face contorted as he realized what Call was doing. Before he could so much as scream, he was gone, pulled into the void. All across the field, his Chaos-ridden howled for him — one long horrible sound that hung over the battlefield. Then they clattered to a stop, like toys whose batteries had sparked and died.

Call glanced toward where Aaron had been, but he was no longer there. He turned to find him, to find someone, but he was having trouble focusing. He felt dizzy and his vision had gone blurry. Slumping down, he felt darkness close in at the edge of his vision. He wasn't sure if he was falling into chaos or into something far deeper.

Stay awake, he ordered himself.

Stay alive.

"Callum!" Master Rufus was saying. "Callum, can you hear me?"

He wasn't sure how much time had passed.

"Call. Please be okay. Please."

It was Tamara and she sounded like she'd been crying, which didn't make sense, since she'd been so mad.

Call tried to speak, tried to tell her that he was okay. He couldn't do it. Maybe he wasn't okay after all.

He cracked his eyes open slightly. Probably too slightly for anyone to notice. His vision was blurred, but he was right: Tamara was leaning over him, and she'd been crying. He wanted to tell her not to cry, but maybe she wasn't crying over him. Maybe she was upset about Havoc. That made more sense. If he'd told her he was okay and she was crying about Havoc, it would have been embarrassing for both of them — especially because he'd probably start crying about Havoc, too.

"You did it," she whispered to him. "You saved everyone. Call, please, please wake up."

At that, he tried harder to move, but he still couldn't. It was as though every part of him was weighted down and even opening an eye fully felt like fighting against that heaviness.

"I'll tell him something that will cheer him up." Jasper's voice came from his other side. Jasper was a dark-haired blur somewhere behind Tamara. If Call could have groaned, he would have. "Call, Celia and I got back together. Isn't that great?"

For a brief moment, Call entertained a brief fantasy that everyone would punch Jasper for him, but no one did. It wasn't fair.

"He's dying," someone said. Master Graves of the Assembly, his dry voice unmistakable. He didn't sound particularly displeased by his announcement. "He used far too much chaos magic for anyone to survive. His soul must be riddled with it now."

Master Rufus turned slowly, and even through the blur Call could see the rage in the look he turned on the other mage. "He did this because of you," Master Rufus said. "You caused this, Graves, and don't think that any of us will forget it."

There was a sniffing sound on Graves's part and then Call heard another voice, closer. Tamara glanced up and stiffened. She didn't move, though, or say anything as another figure drew near. Someone Call recognized despite the blur.

It was Aaron.

Aaron who knelt down beside him. Aaron who put a cool, calm hand on Call's chest.

"I can help him," Aaron said.

"What are you going to do?" Tamara asked. Call wondered if she remembered what she had said to him: that Aaron cared about Call because he had a piece of Call's soul inside him.

Aaron was a blur with a halo of light hair. His voice

sounded firm, almost like the old Aaron. "Call's not supposed to die. I'm the one who should be dead."

Tamara drew in her breath. Call fought to open his eyes wide, fought to say something, to stop Aaron, but then he felt Aaron's hand press against him, and something moved deep in his chest.

Suddenly, there was air to breathe again. Something was moving inside his rib cage. Something with a light touch, like fluttering wings. He felt it brush his soul.

The soul tap. Aaron was doing the soul tap they'd both learned. But how? Aaron wasn't a mage anymore, wasn't a Makar. And why bother? Did he want to know what it was like to feel someone's soul wink out and die?

"What are you doing?" Tamara whispered. "Please don't hurt Call. He's been hurt enough."

Aaron didn't say anything. Call felt it again, the touch deep inside his chest. His injured soul calming. The sense of something being restored to him, something he'd only now known he was missing.

He gasped and his eyes flew open. The blur was gone from his vision. In fact, everything was irradiated with light. His body jerked.

"He's alive," said Master Rufus in amazement. "Call! Call, can you hear me?"

Call nodded; his head hurt, but he was no longer choking and dizzy. He stared up at Aaron. "What did you do?" he demanded.

"I gave you back your soul," Aaron said. "The piece you used to bring me to life. I put it back inside you."

"Aaron," Tamara breathed.

"Tamara," Aaron said. "It's all right." There was a gentleness in his voice Call hadn't heard since Aaron had died. It made him feel like something was expanding inside his chest, something so huge it might crack his ribs open and make him scream. He could almost see the invisible threads connecting him to Aaron — golden, silken-fine threads of soul that stretched between the two of them.

And the opposite of chaos is the human soul.

Master Graves was babbling. "But that's impossible. It can't be done. Souls can't be traded back and forth like — like playing cards!"

Call sat up. The battlefield was thick with smoke. Mages were moving back and forth, putting out fires, rounding up the Chaos-ridden and the traitors. Call saw Jasper's father led away by two burly Assembly mages, though he didn't see Kimiya anywhere.

"So I'm okay?" Call said wonderingly, glancing from Tamara to Aaron to Master Rufus. "We're both okay?"

But Aaron didn't speak. He was very pale. He still had his arms wrapped around himself as if he was cold. "Call," he said breathlessly. His lips were bluish. "It was never supposed to be me. I'm not the hero. You're the hero." Impossibly, he smiled, just the slightest crook of a smile. "It was always you."

"Aaron!" Call cried, but Aaron had slumped down between him and Tamara. Sobbing, she put a hand on Aaron's shoulder and shook him, but under her hand, he was still.

Call felt his own soul thrash desperately toward the golden threads connecting him to Aaron. As though his own soul couldn't bear to let Aaron go. For a moment, the feeling was so intense that Call thought he might pass out again. He concentrated on holding himself together, on pulling in all his energy and his power, on tugging the golden threads to him.

"Aaron's gone," Tamara whispered.

Call opened his eyes. Aaron looked peaceful, lying on the ground. Maybe this was what was best, maybe he was supposed to see it that way, but Call was horrified. The idea of losing him and losing Havoc, too, felt like almost too much to bear.

Call looked around for his wolf, but Havoc was nowhere to be seen. He wasn't where he'd fallen. Had someone moved his body?

He shivered. He wanted his father. He wanted Alastair. He felt gentle hands on him. Master Rufus, holding Call by the shoulders. He hadn't remembered Master Rufus being so gentle, but there was nothing but kindness in his touch as he held Call while a group of mages approached with a stretcher and loaded Aaron's body onto it.

The ache in his chest wouldn't go away. His head buzzed.

There were other groups of mages out on the field, loading

other bodies onto stretchers. "Be careful with him," Call said raggedly, as they raised the stretcher with Aaron on it and began to carry his body away. "Don't hurt him."

"He can't be hurt," Master Rufus said softly. "He's beyond all that, Call."

Tamara was crying softly into her hands. Even Jasper was silent, his face streaked with dirt.

Call wanted to get up and run after the stretcher and grab Aaron off it, to bring him back to his friends. Which was ridiculous, because Aaron was gone. Dead beyond Call's ability to call his soul back, even if he'd been foolish enough to make such a terrible choice twice. But Call wanted to make sure he got a real burial this time.

Even if Call was in prison again, unable to attend it. He thought about the walls of his old cell in the Panopticon. It wouldn't be so bad to be back there now. Maybe it would be restful.

Then he remembered the state they'd left the Panopticon in. Well, he was sure there were other mage jails. Probably one of those would do.

"It's all right, Call," Master Rufus said, as if he could read Call's thoughts. "He will get a hero's funeral. Aaron's name will never be forgotten."

A shadow fell over them all. "Callum, you're going to have to come with me," said Assemblyman Graves. He looked as though he'd been disappointed that Call had pulled through.

"Callum isn't going anywhere," Master Rufus said. "He saved us all and he nearly sacrificed himself to do it. If you try to arrest him, I will encase you in stone. Callum Hunt is a hero, just like Aaron said."

"Yeah," said Tamara. "Touch Callum and I'll burn your fingers off."

Call looked at her in frank amazement. He thought that she understood that he wasn't actually evil, but he figured he'd lost her friendship forever.

But when he gave her a wobbly smile, even though there were tears in her eyes, she smiled back at him.

And then out of the crowd came a barking. Call turned in time for Havoc to bound up to him. Call threw his arms around his wolf's neck and buried his face in the warm fur.

"You're okay," he whispered.

Then he pulled back to make sure. And staring into Havoc's face, he noticed that Havoc's eyes were no longer coruscating. They were a deep, steady gold. The Alkahest must have struck Havoc after all, but instead of killing him, it had taken the chaos from him. Havoc was a regular wolf now.

A regular wolf that licked Call's cheek with a pink tongue.

Master Rufus and Tamara helped Call to his feet. And as the mages flew over the battlefield, putting out fires and arresting the last of the renegade mages, Call and his friends limped toward where Ravan stood like a flaming column beside the other elementals being prepared for the flight back to the Magisterium.

They had almost reached her when Call heard it. A tiny whisper in the back of his head. A voice, fond and curious and friendly, so familiar it seemed to punch a hole right through his chest. So familiar he felt the echo of the soul tap all the way through him, and almost stumbled.

I think I really am back this time, Call, Aaron's voice said. *Now what the heck are we going to do?*

EPILOGUE

I T W A S A bright day, and the sun shone down on a small town cradled by mountains. The town had stood for hundreds of years; its walls were washed by rain and snow to a mellow gold. The light was slanting toward afternoon, and the townspeople were starting to trickle out into the streets to do their evening shopping, when the sound of an enormous explosion split the sky.

In the space between two mountains, above a valley of green grass, the sky seemed to have torn in half, revealing a terrible blackness. It was a darkness more than darkness. It was not a lack of light, but a lack of anything at all. It was the void.

The animals in the valley began to scatter as a rumbling noise came from inside the void. There was a ripping sound, and then from the darkness came Alex Strike, riding on the back of a great metal monster that the mages of the Assembly had once named Automotones.

Alex was no longer human. He had become a thing the world had never seen before. He had become a Devoured of chaos. He was chaos, and chaos lived inside him and flickered behind his black eyes. It crackled in his bones and hair and blood. The silver mask was no longer an independent thing. It had replaced his face, mobile and expressive as his own features had once been.

Behind him flowed a river of elementals and animals that had been once consigned to chaos. There were wolves with coruscating eyes, and dead-eyed mages holding weapons, and the serpent elemental Skelmis hovered over them, hissing and whipping its tail made of air.

Alex rode Automotones to the edge of the valley. He looked down into the town below, where the people were already running in the streets like frightened black ants.

He held out a hand, and in his palm, chaos coiled like smoke.

He smiled.

ABOUT THE AUTHORS

Holly Black and **Cassandra Clare** first met over ten years ago at Holly's first-ever book signing. They have since become good friends, bonding over (among other things) their shared love of fantasy—from the sweeping vistas of *The Lord of the Rings* to the gritty tales of Batman in Gotham City to the classic sword-and-sorcery epics to *Star Wars*. With Magisterium, they decided to team up to write their own story about heroes and villains, good and evil, and being chosen for greatness, whether you like it or not.

Holly is the bestselling author and co-creator of The Spiderwick Chronicles series and won a Newbery Honor for her novel *Doll Bones*. Cassie is the author of bestselling YA series, including The Mortal Instruments, The Infernal Devices, and The Dark Artifices. They both live in Western Massachusetts, about ten minutes away from each other. This is the fourth book in Magisterium, following *The Iron Trial*, *The Copper Gauntlet*, and *The Bronze Key*.